My not-so-terrible Time at the *HIPPIE HOTEL

by

Rosemary Graham

Viking

For reading, listening, and encouraging me along the way: Lou Berney, Shannon Graham Gehrs, Aleta George, Taal Hasak-Lowy, Todd Hasak-Lowy, Susan Hobson, Sarah Kelly, Lesley Quinn, Catherine Shepad-Haier, Denise Simard, Evelyn Strauss, and Ayelet Waldman. Thanks also to Leigh Feldman, teenager at heart, and Elizabeth Law, expert in the teenage head.

VIKING
Published by Penguin Group
Penguin Group (U.S.A.), Inc., 345 Hudson Street, New York, New York 10014, U.S.A.
Penguin Books Ltd, 80 Strand, London WC2R 0RL, England
Penguin Books Australia Ltd, 250 Camberwell Road, Camberwell, Victoria 3124, Australia
Penguin Books Canada Ltd, 10 Alcorn Avenue, Toronto, Ontario, Canada M4V 3B2
Penguin Books (N.Z.) Ltd, 182-190 Wairau Road, Auckland 10, New Zealand

Penguin Books Ltd, Registered Offices: Harmondsworth, Middlesex, England

First published in 2003 by Viking, a division of Penguin Young Readers Group.

1 3 5 7 9 10 8 6 4 2

Copyright © Rosemary Graham, 2003

LIBRARY OF CONGRESS CATALOGING-IN-PUBLICATION DATA
Graham, Rosemary.
My not-so-terrible time at the Hippie Hotel : a young adult novel / by
Rosemary Graham.
p.   cm.
Summary: Forced to go with her father to a house on Cape Cod wheredivorced
parents spend "Together Time" with their kids, teenaged Tracy finds the experience
bearable after meeting a local boy named Kevin.
ISBN 0-670-03611-0 (hardcover)
[1. Divorce—Fiction. 2. Parent and child—Fiction. 3.Vacations—Fiction.
4. Friendship—Fiction.] I. Title.
PZ7.G7558 My 2003
[Fic]—dc21
2002015753

Printed in U.S.A.
Set in Sabon
Designed by Kelley McIntyre

*

To Kevin, in real life

*

Farnsworth House

Sharon Farnsworth Hopkins, Proprietor ✦ Falmouth, Massachusetts

Hank Forrester
201 E. 71st St., Apt. 15G
New York, NY 10021

May 15, 2000

Dear Hank,

This is to confirm your family's participation in the Farnsworth House Summer 2000 Together Time. I've reserved a private room for you, and space for your children in the dormitories. My understanding is that you will be accompanied by your son, Chris, fifteen, and your daughters, Tracy, fourteen, and Emmy, six.

We have two other families joining us this summer, among whom I trust your kids will find some buddies. Loraine Panetta, from Manhattan, will be coming with her fifteen-year-old daughter, Beka, and her six-year-old twins, Sammi, a girl, and Sean, a boy. Larry Wilcox, of Cambridge, will bring his daughter Kelsey, fifteen, and his son, Josh, who's ten. The children live with their mother in Berkeley, California.

As a divorced parent, I know how emotionally charged the prospect of a "family vacation" can be for parents and kids affected by divorce. My son Paul (now seventeen) and I created Together Time with the idea that the old-fashioned family vacation could be reinvented to serve the needs of today's divorced families. Guests share meals—as well as meal preparation and clean-up—and travel together for sight-seeing excursions and other outdoor adventures. I believe these group activities comfort younger children, who may be missing the absent parent, as well as adolescents, who may feel stigmatized as members of "incomplete" families.

An invoice is enclosed. The cost of meals and admissions fees to sight-seeing destinations is included in the price of your stay. You can send me a check now, or pay in full on your arrival.

I've been spending summers at Farnsworth House since I was a child. It is, if I may be so bold, a magical place, a place that nurtures the heart and the soul. Many lifelong friendships have begun under its roof.

Sincerely,

Sharon Farnsworth Hopkins

✳Chapter 1✳

I don't know if it was the whispers or the squeaking bedsprings, but something made me open my eyes at exactly 12:13 A.M. Staring at the red digits, I felt that where-am-I? you get when you wake up in the middle of the night in a bed that isn't yours in a place that doesn't smell like home. Musty, with a hint of ocean. Oh yeah. I remembered. Once I figured out where I was, I knew the voices and squeaks had to be coming from a certain bed across the room.

Or maybe what woke me up was my little sister Emmy talking in her sleep. She does that a lot at home, too.

What she said, just as I was coming to, was "Paul," which was weird, because I was pretty sure that the person on the bed with the girl across the room—who could only be Beka, because it was her bed—was a guy named Paul.

After Emmy said that, they got quiet for what seemed like forever. Then Emmy said something all mumbly, but with a very clear "fried clams" in the middle, which I thought was pretty funny, and which let them know she was dreaming. Slowly the bed springs started up again. The two people across the room resumed their activity without realizing that they had indeed been discovered, not by Emmy but by me.

I wasn't sure what I had discovered though, because I couldn't see them from the position I lay in, and if I rolled over, my cot would squeak, too, and they'd surely look my way, and I didn't know if I could pull off the fake sleep thing. So all I had to go on was what I could hear.

He said: "Here?"

She said: "Yeah."

Then quiet.

He said: "Mmm. Cool."

She said: "How about this?"

Quiet.

He said, "That's great."

She said: "Shhh!" And giggled.

Paul works here at Farnsworth House, the place my father calls the Hippie Hotel, because it's run by Paul's mother Sharon, a tie-dye-and-Birkenstock-wearing woman whose gray hair is so long it almost reaches her butt. Dad took us—me, Emmy, and our brother

Chris—on this weird vacation. It's called "Together Time." The Web site promises "single parents and their children an old-fashioned family vacation among other families in a historic, rambling cottage by the sea."

I think the idea is that if you get divorced kids together with other divorced kids, they won't feel so bad about being divorced.

So far it hasn't worked.

You should see the other "families" here. Aside from Sharon and Paul, and my dad and us, there's just one right now, made up of Loraine Panetta, who talks and smokes all the time, her fifteen-year-old daughter Beka—the one on the bed with Paul—and her six-year-old twins Sammi (a girl) and Sean (a boy).

Since Beka and I are so close in age, you might think, as I thought before I met her, that there would be some friend potential. But there isn't. We're different. Way different.

First of all, she lives in New York and goes to private school. I live in the suburbs and go to a big public high school. Those two facts in and of themselves should tell you a lot.

Beka is one of those New York private school girls who's taken so many ballet lessons that she stands and walks with her feet permanently turned out in second position. She's punk, though, not princess. She's got the all-black wardrobe, the eyeliner, the jet-black dyed hair. She smokes too, which every New York private school girl—punk or princess—does, and which probably helps her stay as skinny as she is. She hates her mother and flirts with all the guys in the house, including my brother and my father, as well as Paul, even though Paul's the only one she really wants.

Beka, Emmy, Sammi, and I had been sleeping in the "girls' dormitory"—Sharon's fancy name for an attic room with a bunch of mismatched twin beds, futons, and squeaky cots—for three nights, but all Beka had said to me was stuff like, "There's no eating allowed up here, you know." As if she was the big rule follower. And, "Excuse me, excuse me, can I get by?" in a way that implied I was too big to walk around, which, while I admit to putting on a few pounds lately, is still a huge, mean exaggeration. And, "Brett Smith? You still listen to *Brett Smith*?" when she flipped through my CD carrier the first night without asking.

Okay. As you've probably gathered, I am not skinny. Aside from that, I can't dance. I don't smoke. I can't even talk to—never mind flirt with—boys my age. And yes, I listen to Brett Smith.

I listen to Brett Smith even though she is now one of the top-selling recording artists of all time. Even though some of her fans are as young as eleven. Even though you can't go for a twenty-minute car ride without hearing her on the radio, or watch *TRL* without seeing her latest video. I listened to her before any of this happened, back when I was twelve and my

Uncle Steve bought me her debut CD to encourage me with my piano. And I'm not going to stop listening to her now, just because all these other people know how good she is, now that she's no longer got the cult thing going on, and now that she's rich. Besides, I happen to know that she gives a lot of her money away to shelters for runaway girls and arts programs in inner-city schools.

Beka prefers cutting-edge punk bands with cult followings. She's always trying to get my brother Chris to listen to some CD or other of a band she knows from "The Village" or heard about through her punk connections on the Internet.

I don't smoke. Not that I'm such a goody-goody or anything. It's just that it makes me sick, literally. The first time I tried—at the beginning of eighth grade—I almost threw up, and the second time I tried—at the end of eighth grade—I did throw up. And so I haven't tried since.

Dancing I wish I could do, but I can't. This is not a low self-esteem thing. I really cannot dance. To begin with, I don't have a dancer's body. At least not a skinny ballerina dancer's body like Beka's. I'm not exactly fat, though I've been close over the last year or so. Anyway it's not just about size. My friend Zann dragged me to one of her hip-hop classes where there were lots of unskinny girls who could really move. I just can't get the music to come out my legs and feet.

Which is kind of funny, because I'm pretty good at getting it to come out my fingers. I can play piano by ear. If I hear something a few times, I can figure out how to get my fingers to make the sounds on the piano. That's my one talent. I write songs, too, and I might be good at that. I'm not sure because I've only played them for Uncle Steve, who says I'm very good, but who's obviously biased.

It doesn't matter right now because I'm on strike.

My dad and I used to have this Saturday morning routine of bagels and coffee (decaf, with lots of cream and sugar for me) before driving over to Mrs. Finch's for my lesson. After the divorce, he tried to keep it up for a while, but he would get stuck in traffic, or have an important, sudden business meeting at his new job, and my mom would have to take me early, so that she could get Chris to soccer, and I'd have to wait in Mrs. Finch's front parlor through two other kids' half-hour lessons and then take a bus home.

Nobody actually knows about the strike. I told my mom and dad and Mrs. Finch that I just wanted to take a little break, that the pressure of keeping up with piano was getting to me with all the added responsibilities of starting high school. Mrs. Finch freaked and made me promise to come see her in September "to reassess." My parents both seemed kind of baffled, but they didn't inquire any further so they don't know that I'm on strike. They just think

I'm making my own choices, which is a big part of their parental philosophy. Plus they've both been pretty distracted since the divorce.

So I haven't gotten a chance to make my demands the way striking workers do. I'm not even sure what I would demand if I got that chance. It's not like things are going to go back to the way they were just because I stop playing piano. And "back to the way they were" isn't exactly what my first choice would be.

Anyway, you'd think that if I had this natural ability to hear music and make it come out my fingers and make the piano do what I wanted it to, that maybe I could get my feet to do something simple like follow the beat. But there's no way.

Beka's good. I walked in on her while she was dancing in the game room our first night here. She had Madonna's "Music" cranked up really loud, so she didn't know I was in the room. She was doing this routine from the video, and I swear, it was like she had choreographed it herself or something. She had every last move down, even the turns of the head and the flip of the hair, only her hair didn't quite flip like Madonna's. It's too frizzy.

So despite our being close in age, and having grown up within thirty miles of each other, and having shared the challenges of being *Children of Divorce*, Beka and I had nothing to talk about at the Farnsworth House Together Time and had so far spent most of our time as far apart as possible, which is pretty far when you consider how many rooms this rambling cottage by the sea has.

But we had to sleep in the same room. All children sixteen and under had to sleep in the dormitories. The girls in the attic and the boys at the back of the second floor, where the parents can check on them, and where there's no way to get to the girls' dorm without walking past all of the parents' rooms. But Paul's got his own room, since this is basically his house and he works here all summer, and maybe also because he just turned seventeen. It's downstairs next to the kitchen, which is next to the pantry, which luckily for him and Beka I guess, has a set of "secret stairs," as Sharon insists on calling them, even though everyone knows about them, that were built so the servants could go up and down to their quarters in the attic without disturbing the snotty olden-day residents.

Beka's sister Sammi is okay. She and my sister, Emmy, who just turned six, are friends. They build sand cities on the beach during the day and put on shows at night with these moldy old Beanie Babies they found in a closet. Sean plays with them sometimes, but mostly he likes to do things like pretend he's a tornado and knock down their creations or play the big bad wolf, the mean old troll, or even the witch if there are no bad "boy parts" for him to act out. He yells, roars, knocks things over. Whatever the story, he's the agent of destruction, gobbling up the three Beanie Baby pigs, or Beanie Baby Riding Hood, knocking down the sand castle or the shopping mall the girls spent hours putting together. Earlier in the day I'd seen him off by himself smashing a dead horseshoe crab against the rocks on the jetty. He held it by the pointy horn and just whacked away, over and over, until the shell was broken into about a hundred pieces and the poor dead crab's stick legs were strewn all over the sand. While he did this, his mother, Loraine, sat on her towel staring out at the water, once in a while letting out a big sigh, and a half-hearted "Don't do that, honey. It's not nice."

My fifteen-year-old brother Chris thinks he's friends with Beka. They go off smoking together after dinner when we're supposed to be gaming it up in the game room.

Farnsworth House has no television because, as Sharon explained the night we arrived, "Farnsworth House is committed to fostering community among its guests." She says, "You might all be in the same room while you're watching TV, but you're not interacting with each other." Which to me is the whole point of television—not having to talk to the other people in the room.

Down in the mildewy basement there's a radio and CD player, a ping-pong table, a pool table with an almost complete set of balls but only one stick that you have to pass around, and a computer so old it doesn't even have a modem or a CD-drive. All you can do is Minesweeper or Pac-Man. There's a closet full of old board games: Monopoly, Life, and Scrabble, all with pieces, cards, and directions missing, and yellowed score sheets from previous prisoners of the Hippie Hotel.

So I can't say I blame Chris and Beka for heading behind the house for a cigarette instead. I might have done the same thing if I smoked. I worry though, that Beka's going to mess things up for Chris. He's kind of on probation with our parents, because of his report card and because he and his friend Dean got caught skipping school. He has to "earn back his freedom" by showing he can make "responsible choices." Being—or trying to be—friends with Beka seems pretty irresponsible to me.

I worry, too, that Chris might be hoping for more than friendship from her. And there's just no way. Chris is skinny, scrawny-skinny, and only about up to her eyebrows. Paul on the other hand is seventeen, going into his junior year. He's tall, and has a deep, Baywatch tan. But there's nothing lifeguardy about him. He's got short, spiky blond hair and three tiny diamond studs in one ear. When he's not working around Farnsworth House, he's up the street at the local school playground, skateboarding with his friends. He's really good.

Chris and I and Emmy are a family of pale, freckly redheads who burn easily. We get that from our mother, who's all Irish. Summer is not our best season, lookswise. Chris tried to pierce his own ear a few months ago but it got infected. The hole turned all red and oozy, and the doctor said it had to be left to close.

Chris is just someone Beka passes the time with when Paul's busy cooking our meals and painting the deck and stuff during the day.

*   *   *

It's weird to be awake while two people are on a bed across the room from you doing something that involves little talking and a lot of spring squeaking. Finally, after lying there for what seemed like forever, my curiosity got to me. I had to look. First I moved one foot, then an elbow, and then, as slowly as I could, my neck and head. I kept my mouth closed and breathed a little more loudly than normal through my nose, like sleeping people do. Then, one at a time, I lifted my eyelids just enough to see out of, but not enough to look like I was awake.

Thanks to the moonbeams coming in through the skylight, I could make out that they were not making out. They were, in fact, sitting up, fully clothed. Their heads were really close together, but they were not kissing.

I couldn't figure out what they were doing until I heard a click and saw Beka lean over toward the nightstand next to her bed. The moonlight flashed on something shiny and silver. A CD. They were both plugged into the Walkman she carried everywhere and which she would be plugged into all the time if her mother didn't tell her to take it off now and then.

She said, "You've got to hear this one cut."

He said, "Cool."

Aha.

*   *   *

I must have fallen back to sleep, because the next thing I knew the red numbers said 1:38 and the room was completely quiet. The moonlight shone on Beka, alone now, asleep in the artfully torn-up Brady Bunch T-shirt she wore every day. Funny how different she looked all still like that. Without her signature black eyeliner and the perma-sneer she wore during waking hours, she looked like she could be nice.

I was pretty sure I was the only awake person in Farnsworth House now. I could hear the tiny waves of Nantucket Sound hitting the beach out front, and I tried for a while to concentrate on the rhythmic plishing and swishing, hoping to be lulled back to sleep. But I just couldn't relax. I closed my eyes and pictured the little waves lapping the shore, and the tiny shells and rocks swirling just below the water's surface. But then I'd start to think about Sharon's amazingly well-stocked pantry just below me, with shelves full of industrial-sized chips, cookies, and cereals. Only one empty bed stood between me and the secret stairs that led to unguarded, unlimited snackage.

I made my way to the stairs, which are very narrow, and held my arms out to either side, using the walls for balance. I took one at a time, being careful not to put my full weight down, which would make the old wood creak.

I knew exactly where to find the M&M's.

Of course the peanut were easier to spot in the dark because of the bright yellow bag. I wanted plain, though, the pure chocolate melt-in-your-mouth thing. Here I faced a dilemma. A half-full one-pound bag, with the empty part neatly folded down and clipped shut with a clothespin, stood in front of three full, unopened bags. I stood for a minute, asking myself what was more likely to get noticed if someone happened to be paying attention to the M&M inventory on the shelves of the Farnsworth House pantry: the present, open bag going down by another half and left folded and sealed as before, or the disappearance of one whole, unopened bag?

Stealing food is kind of a hobby of mine. But I'm a little out of practice since my mother's stopped keeping anything worth raiding the kitchen for around. She said she didn't care which one of us was doing it, she just wasn't going to buy treats anymore. That was after a particularly bad night, when I'd only intended to eat one or two Ho Hos and wound up eating all twelve in a fresh box. It had taken me about an hour, unwrapping each one, biting off the hard chocolate coating first, then unrolling it to lick the white frosting. I wasn't going to bother with the spongy chocolate cake, but after all the frosting and cream was gone, I ate that, too. By the time I'd finished the last one, it was nearly morning, and I'd stumbled back to bed, the blue-and-silver foil wrappers crumpled into a single ball which I hid under my pillow, and slept till noon.

Everyone knows it's me. I guess it's what you might call an open secret in our family. In the year since our parents' divorce was final I've gained fifteen pounds, while Chris and Emmy have stayed skinny. They complain that it isn't fair to punish them, but my mother says it's better for everyone to eat healthier snacks. She bought a case of granola bars at Costco. They're okay when you're actually hungry, but I'm not tempted to sneak them away under cover of darkness or anything.

I decided to go for the whole bag, thinking that Sharon would be more likely to assume she had miscounted the bags than to forget from one day to the next how many M&M's she put in the trail mix. A pound would come in handy for the rest of the week, I told myself, wondering whether it would last past the next day.

Cradling the bag in my arm, I walked through the kitchen and dining room and into the room Sharon calls the parlor. I sat for a minute at the bench of the old upright piano against the wall under the main stairs. Above it were all these old photographs of Farnsworth

House history. In one, a young woman dressed in a high-collared, tight-waisted long dress sat playing the piano and singing. Maybe I should say "girl." She might have been twenty or twenty-five or seventeen for all I knew. Old black-and-white pictures and old clothes make everyone look old to me. Anyway, her eyes were closed and her mouth was open in a little "o." A group of bearded men in vests and women in those same high-collared dresses stood around listening and smiling. During our obligatory first-day tour and history lesson, Sharon told us that the girl turned out to be a famous songwriter who wrote for Broadway musicals.

I put the M&M's down next to me for a minute and ran my fingers over the keys, being careful not to press down. I touched out a verse of Brett Smith's "Summergirl," and for a moment, I totally forgot about eating and about the fact that I had renounced the piano.

Then I spied my bag of loot and took it out to the sunporch.

When we were younger, Mom used to buy big bags of M&M's for Saturday nights when she and Dad went to the movies. This was before Emmy was born. She'd set up three plastic bowls, one for Chris, one for me, and one for our babysitter. Chris and I would divide ours up by color and then use them for betting while we played Go Fish.

Somehow, my brother learned how to identify the color of an M&M blindfolded. They all taste alike to me, but then again, I've never been able to eat them like he does: one at a time, sucking all the color off, then biting into the chocolate when it's mushy warm.

I dumped half the bag out on the old, stained wooden table and started to separate the colors, thinking about the old days when my family didn't have to go to some weird hotel on Cape Cod to be together, wondering if it was true what Zann said about green M&M's making you horny, when I smelled cigarette smoke mixed in with the salt air coming through the windows. I looked out to see two shadowy figures walking up from the water toward the house.

One was Loraine—impossible not to recognize her frizzy hair. And I knew that if one was her, the other had to be my father. She'd been stalking him since we got here, sitting next to him at meals and starting these really obvious let's-get-to-know-each-other conversations every chance she got.

My father's very smart and handsome and funny, and what you would call successful. He works in telecommunications, setting up wireless phone systems across the world. Even though he's already had a couple of girlfriends since the divorce, and even though I know it's totally normal, I can't get used to seeing him so much as talk to women who aren't my mother.

The first time he brought us to his new apartment in New York—this was about a month after he moved out—I saw a bra in his laundry hamper and I almost threw up. I don't know why I even looked in there except I seem to be unable *not* to look in places where there might be things I'm not supposed to see.

Before Loraine and my father made it up the steps to the front door, I moved into a dark corner of the sunporch where Sharon had tried unsuccessfully to get us all to play charades the first night.

"No, it's true, scout's honor," I heard Loraine say as they walked through the front door. They were whispering, but still, she was loud. She was holding up three fingers of one hand and had the other over her heart like she was taking an oath. I couldn't hear what my father said in response, but Loraine laughed, and the two of them disappeared up the stairs to the private parental rooms.

I listened really hard, but I only heard one door shut. It might have been two doors shutting at the same time. But it would have had to be at *exactly* the same time to sound like it sounded.

✳*Chapter* **2**✳

"Tracy! Traceee! Dad says to get up."

Emmy was pulling at my feet. I'd been smelling pancakes and coffee and hearing kitchen noises for a while, but I had no interest in breakfast. All I wanted was sleep.

I could still feel the M&M's in my stomach. I imagined them in one big pile: red, yellow, green oozing together in a big brown mess. It would be hours before I could eat. But was I thirsty.

"Tell him I'm getting up. I just want juice anyway."

A few minutes later my father called up from the pantry, "Tracy, we're leaving for Provincetown in ten minutes."

He poked his head in from the stairs. "Come on honey, rise and shine. Loraine and I thought it would be fun to take everyone down to the edge of the world. You'll love it there."

Uck. I'd been afraid something like this was going to happen. A day trip with that slutty, frizzy-haired woman and her slutty, frizzy-haired daughter.

*   *   *

Forty-five minutes later I was sharing a seat belt with my sister in the station wagon my Dad rented for our so-called family so-called vacation. The twins were in the way back, and Beka and my brother were on the other side of Emmy, plugged into Beka's Walkman, listening to some band she's supposed to know back in New York. She had the Brady Bunch shirt on again. She'd drawn a mustache on Marcia and a goatee on Bobby since yesterday, when she'd only had Mrs. Brady's eyes blacked out and a cigarette dangling from Cindy's lips. The T-shirt's supposed to show us how "irreverent" Beka is. She uses that word like five times a day.

Dad and Loraine were listening to public radio, an interview with some writer Loraine was supposed to know in college. I extended my ears as far as possible to try to pick up on their conversation. I'm a snoop. I'm totally incapable of not listening to other people's conversations when they're within earshot. In fact I have considerably more muscular control over my ears than the average person. I can literally bend my ears.

"He was always very ambitious," I heard her tell my father. "I never thought his writing was all that remarkable, but he was driven. I guess that's served him well. Of course it can't hurt that he's married to Juliana Hale."

It was a name I'd never heard, and from his raised eyebrow, I gathered my father hadn't either. "Juliana Hale?" said Loraine, in a tone that reminded me of Beka's "You still listen to Brett Smith?" Only since Loraine was trying to impress my father, not put him down, it wasn't quite so snotty. "The literary agent?"

Dad shrugged.

"Michael Snow? Rachel Schilling?" Okay, he nodded, he knew who they were. Even I knew who they were, or at least the names sounded familiar. "Juliana Hale is the biggest literary agent in New York."

Loraine went on to tell Dad about how she had wanted to be a writer when she was in college, but "things hadn't worked out." When she said that, she sort of nodded her head back over her shoulder, as if to say her kids had gotten in the way of her dreams of fame and fortune. Now she was stuck teaching English and creative writing at Bellwin, the fancy private school Beka went to, hoping to get back to her own writing "someday."

Emmy interrupted my surveillance mission to complain that the seat belt was too tight. "It's cutting into my stomach," she whined. "Why can't I have my own seat? Why couldn't we take two cars?"

"When are we going to get there?" asked Sean.

"I wanna get out of this car!" yelled Sammi.

"Quiet!" yelled Beka, even louder than everyone else, since she had headphones on and couldn't hear herself.

Loraine looked annoyed and apologetic at the same time, but didn't say anything. Instead, she looked to my father, who did his best to distract everyone.

"We're coming up to the dunes. Over on your left."

My father spent all of his summers on Cape Cod as a kid. When Chris and I were little, we went there every summer until our grandparents sold their cottage and moved to Florida. We've got pictures at home of everyone in plastic lobster bibs. In one, my father's holding a huge red lobster up to his mouth, like he's going to bite into it, antennae and all. My mother sits next to him, her hand on his back, and she's laughing so hard it looks like she's going to pee in her pants.

Every time we passed a sign for a different beach he started another story about what he and his brothers did when they were kids and teenagers, like capsizing in a little motorboat and having to get rescued by the Coast Guard. As we approached Truro, the town just below Provincetown, he started on the dunes. He'd been talking about the dunes for weeks, since he first signed us up for the Together Time experience.

I could kind of see what he meant. There's not much out there but a lot of white sand and an occasional shack. You can't build anything there now, because the government took over and made it National Seashore, but a few old places have been allowed to stay.

Beka and Chris didn't hear any of Dad's lecture. She was closing her eyes and moving her shoulders up and down, back and forth, grooving to her friend's brother's friend's band. Chris watched her and pretended to listen, moving his head just enough to let her know he thought it was cool, too. Sean kept insisting he saw whales out at sea, ignoring everyone who tried to tell him they didn't swim that close to shore.

*   *   *

We had to park a mile or so outside of "P-town" (as my father kept calling it to show Loraine he was hip) and take a rumbly, smelly bus. The old bus driver let us out next to a set of stairs that led to an alley, which, he explained, would take us out to Commercial Street.

"That's where all the fun is. If you want to go whale watching, the boats are down behind Commercial Street. You kids have a nice time now. And don't get lost. Provincetown is no place for kids to get lost in." Then he looked at Dad and Loraine like did they know what they were doing?

One of the first things we saw in that alley was a man dressed in tight leather pants with boots that went up to his knees. He wasn't wearing a shirt, and he had gold rings through both nipples. There was a big whale tattoo on one arm, and he had one of those mustaches that goes all the way out to big fuzzy sideburns.

Before the guy was quite out of earshot Sammi said, "He must be really hot in those pants."

And Emmy started to ask, "Why did that man have *earrings* on his—"

But Dad cut her off, all camp-counselor-like, "Okayyy. . . .What does everyone want for lunch? Hamburgers? Lobster rolls? Clams?"

All three, on one plate, as soon as possible, for me.

My father's diversion tactic worked. The guy turned a corner, and Dad continued in the camp-counselor mode, "Emmy, Sammi, Sean. Provincetown is a place where some people come to express themselves. They're on vacation, and they want to relax. For some people, that means dressing up. Or down, as the case may be. . . ."

He snuck a look at Loraine when he said that, and she gave him one of those knowing, admiring smiles.

"Like when we do 'Halloween in July' at camp?"

"Yeah, like that," he said, relieved, again sneaking a look at Loraine who I think may have actually batted an eyelash. "The important thing for us as guests here is to keep our comments and questions to ourselves."

At which point Chris turned to Beka and said, "But that's got to hurt." Meaning, I assume, the nipples. I was about to say something like, "Yeah, you should know," so that I could embarrass him by bringing up the bungled ear-piercing episode, but the thought of Beka and Paul on her bed the night before stopped me. There'd be enough pain down the line for Chris this vacation. I didn't have to add to it.

*   *   *

Loraine nixed the first restaurant we looked at, because, she said, "I feel like a salad."

I thought I was going to faint when Dad said, "That's funny, you don't look like a salad."

Emmy's mouth kind of dropped, and she looked at me. I looked at Chris, who looked at Dad, who looked guilty, almost like he couldn't believe he did it either.

It was an old family joke between him and Mom. He'd say it every time she said "I feel like a . . ." whatever. And we'd all kid him for making the same stupid joke over and over again. But it was fun, you know? One of those things that made us *us*. I could tell, too, that even though Loraine smiled, the lame joke gave her second thoughts about Dad's man-of-her-dreams possibilities.

Walking up to the menu posted in another restaurant window, Dad bellowed out, "Here we go, here we go. Clams, burgers, and . . . zee sa-lade for ma-dame." Oh no. He was doing the French accent. Just when I thought things couldn't get any more uncomfortable, he started in on another family joke. Family as in him and Mom and us. Not Loraine and Beka and devilspawn Sean, and Sammi, even though she was nice and cute.

"I want a milkshake. Do they have milkshakes?" Emmy didn't really care about the milkshake; she just wanted attention.

"Can I have a milkshake, Mom?" asked Sammi.

"If *she* gets a milkshake, *I* get a milkshake," Sean yelled in a way I thought deserved a time-out, or at least a warning.

"We don't usually *do* milkshakes," Loraine said to my dad, who had picked up Emmy and was saying, at that exact moment: "Of course you can have a milk-shake, princess. We're on vacation. You can have three milkshakes if you want."

Sean's eyes widened, and he whipped his head back to look at Loraine. "I want three milkshakes," he said, just daring her to say no.

Loraine hesitated, looked around at all of us waiting for her answer, and said, "Well, maybe you and your sister and I can share a milkshake."

"I want my *own* milkshake," Sean insisted.

"Yeah, me too. I want my *own*. We're on vacation," echoed Sammi.

Loraine threw her hands up. "Okay, okay. We're on vacation."

I thought I saw her upper lip curl up a bit as she

looked over at my father one last time before heading into the restaurant. Beka, who had been looking across the street and pointing and talking with Chris, grabbed Loraine's hand just as she stepped through the open door.

"Can Chris and I go over there for lunch?" She tilted her head toward a place with an outdoor grill and a bunch of wooden picnic tables packed into rows. A reggae band played on a patio overlooking the water.

The parents exchanged looks and shrugs, and Dad handed Chris two twenty dollar bills, and even though I hated both of them I wished I could go, too. Anything to avoid watching Loraine move in on my dad. "Be back here in exactly forty-five minutes. And I want change," he added, pointing to the crisp twenties in my brother's hand.

So then we were six, instead of eight, not that it made a difference since the hostess told us we'd have to wait at least a half hour for a table, which would probably be the case anywhere "this time of day, this time of year."

And so we stood in the crowded entryway of Captain Ahab's Fish'n Burgers, watching as tray after tray packed full of fried clams and french fries, cheeseburgers and milkshakes passed by on their way to other people's tables, other people's mouths. By the time we were seated, the M&M's were just a guilty memory. I was hungry.

Emmy started saying, "Burger and a shake, burger and a shake," over and over again, shaking her legs back and forth like she used to do when she was really little and excited or worried. She'd latch onto something like "Read a book" and repeat it until it sounded like one word: "Readabook, readabook." She was sitting there, in a kind of trance saying, "Burger and shake burger and shake burgerandshake," moving her legs back and forth, when the waiter finally came to take our order.

Dad started. "My daughter will have a cheese-burger—"

"*Hamburger.*"

"But I thought—"

A few weeks before, Emmy had announced to me and Chris and my mom that she no longer liked cheeseburgers. This was news to Dad.

"*Hamburgerhamburger!*" she yelled. Shaking faster and faster.

"Okay. Hamburger and chocolate—"

"*Vanillavanillavanilla.*"

He'd also missed the switch from chocolate to vanilla.

"A *vanilla* shake for Princess Emmy. And I'll have the lobster roll."

He was doing his best to act normal, like nothing really remarkable was happening. Loraine kept shooting looks at Emmy, so I started shooting looks at Sean who was going on and on to no one in particular about how Captain Ahab had a wooden leg because a whale "ate it off. In one bite! Crunch. Crunch. Just like that, and there was blood everywhere gushing over everyone. . . ."

Doing her best to ignore her monster-child, Loraine asked, "What kind of lettuce do you use in your Cobb salad?"

"Umm . . . green?" The waiter was probably fifteen. It looked like he had about ten other tables to take care of. *Hello? Loraine? We're not in New York anymore.*

"Oh, never mind, never mind," she said waving her hand in front of the gigantic laminated menu. "Bring me the Cobb salad. Hold the bacon and the blue cheese and put the dressing on the side."

I ordered a lobster roll with fries, passing up the healthier choice of the side salad and ignoring the eyebrow that went up on Loraine's forehead. Then, just to get back at that eyebrow, I added a strawberry shake.

Once the food was ordered, the little kids calmed down and started coloring their "Wonders of the Sea" place mats. With nothing better to do, I took the yellow crayon out of Emmy's mini box and began working on her starfish. I decided I would get through this little field trip to hell by giving myself distracting tasks like this. I went very slowly, keeping all my strokes in one direction, maintaining a light, even pressure throughout. If I had to be the only fourteen-year-old in the whole state of Massachusetts spending what should have been valuable vacation time coloring Stanley the Starfish, at least I would do it well.

I was eyeing Oscar the Octopus, thinking he might look good in purple, when Chris rushed up to our table. He was out of breath, and he looked scared. "Beka's in trouble."

* * *

Three hours later, we were driving back to Hyannis. This time Chris and Emmy were sharing the seat belt on one side of me, while Beka sat on the other, sulking and staring out the window. Sean and Sammi were asleep in the way back. No one was talking.

It wasn't that big a deal, but it did involve officers of the law. She had been trying to buy a drink with a fake ID. And the P-town police were cracking down, since there'd been a bad drunk driving incident earlier in the summer involving teenagers. At the police station, Dad went with Loraine into a room behind the front desk while we ate soggy lunches out of Styrofoam containers. When Dad and Loraine came out, like a half hour later, Beka was with them, looking meaner than ever. We were going home. Beka would get a warning, not a citation. One of the cops smiled at us as we all piled out the front door, saying, "Don't be in such a rush to grow up, kid. You got plenty of time."

Beka ignored him, but I looked back. He had one of those strong New England accents that made him sound older than he looked, which I'd say was mid-thirties. He winked at me. In a nice way—not sleazy or anything. "Someday you'll be wishing you could erase the years." Beka just grunted. So I smiled at him. But I could kind of see her point. I mean, what did he think, Beka was just gonna go, "You know, you're right, I really should slow down and smell the roses and the coffee and the bacon because some day I'll be old and wonder where all the flowers and the coffee and the bacon have gone. I won't take that drink today officer, I'll wait six years, till it's legal."

*　　*　　*

Finally, Loraine broke the silence of our drive. "You know that cop was right. Couldn't you just slow it down a little? Honestly. You just had to have a vodka tonic in the middle of the afternoon? Vodka tonic? I haven't seen one of those since the early eighties. And what about your medication?"

"Mom!"

"What?"

"Can't I have a little privacy, please? I mean, do you have to broadcast everything to people we don't even know?" As she said that she looked around the car at me and Dad and even Chris, who pretended not to notice and turned his head back out the window.

"Well, miss missy. If you want privacy, maybe you should stop breaking the law. Law-abiding citizens have plenty of privacy." Loraine was really mad. Now it didn't seem like she cared about what my father thought or about how she looked or about how many calories were in anything. "Maybe your father was right. Maybe you should live with him for a while."

"Oh right. High school in Wisconsin. You think you can make me into some kind of Little House on the Prairie girl just by putting me on a plane? It doesn't work that way, you know? I can't stand being there for two weeks. I'd *die* if you made me live in Wisconsin. Die. Kill myself if I had to. With a razor blade. Maybe poison."

Loraine glared at Beka. I'm not sure I'd ever seen a look quite like it before. Loraine was angry. Really pissed. But she looked scared, too. Like she didn't know what to do. "We'll talk about this later." And then she turned back around and stared out the window.

For the next hour, no one said a word. Loraine seemed to lose all interest in my father, who didn't seem to notice. He was too busy hitting the SEEK button on the radio, over and over again, saying, "Come on. There's got to be someone in Massachusetts who cares about the Yankees."

* * *

When we pulled up to Farnsworth House, a big, dark blue SUV with a roof rack and three shiny new trail bikes sat in the circular driveway.

"Aha, new arrivals," Dad said, as if this news was going to cheer everyone up.

"Oh great," muttered Beka, "new freaks for the Farnsworth Family Freak Show."

Chapter 3

A thin, muscular, dad-aged guy emerged from the front door and waved. He wore shiny black cycling shorts and a bright yellow Tour de France shirt packed with logos and pockets in weird places. He had bulging cyclist calves, and he was very tan. By the time my dad opened his car door, the new guy was standing there, hand extended for the man-to-man greeting.

"Larry Wilcox."

"Hank Forrester."

"Here for one last fling as a single dad," Larry said, as he walked over to the SUV and pulled a bright green-and-yellow suitcase out of the back.

* * *

Fifteen minutes later the owner of that suitcase, fifteen-year-old Kelsey Wilcox, and I were up in the dorm exchanging life stories. She unrolled a bright green sleeping bag and put her clothes in the old chest of drawers at the end of her bed. Everything she owned was either the same bright green as her suitcase, bright orange, or bright pink, with a little creamy yellow here and there. She had five different pairs of chunky flip-flops, all in varying combinations of those colors.

"What was that about a last fling?"

"Oh. Dad's getting married in the fall. Or remarried, I guess I should say. To Carolyn, about whom I'm trying to think good thoughts. That's my grandmother's idea. She hasn't actually met Carolyn, so she thinks it's all a matter of my attitude. She thinks it's just your typical daughter not liking the new wife thing. Anyway, my grandmother's the one who came up with the idea of one last pre-wedding, just-us-and-Dad vacation. And Carolyn was fine with it because she doesn't want Dad butting into her plans for the perfect wedding."

I looked at the old drawers, the droopy beds, the threadbare rugs. "Why'd he pick this place?"

"Actually, he wanted to take us to Hawaii, which Josh and I were all for, but Mim—that's what we call my grandmother—talked him into this instead. She's a therapist, and she read about it on some Web site. She thought it would be a good bonding opportunity."

After the last tank top was put away, Kelsey pulled out a bag of what looked like Tootsie Pops, but with wrappers in the same bright green, orange, pink, and yellow as her clothes.

"Want one?" she asked, unwrapping a green one and popping it in her mouth. "They're Mexican. Chula Pops."

"Sure."

I chose pink, which tasted like strawberry ice cream. I had to concentrate on eating it normally—sucking, licking slowly instead of biting down just as soon as it hit my mouth, like I would if I were alone—as Kelsey explained her family.

She and Josh lived in Berkeley, California, with their mother and grandparents. She used to live in Boston, but her mom decided to go to law school back in Berkeley, where she grew up, after her divorce.

"She says now it's her turn. She supported my dad through business school, stayed home with us while we were young, and now she's going to be her own person. Dad's in real estate—commercial real estate—and Mom got a big settlement."

I was amazed at how matter-of-factly Kelsey talked about her parents' split, like it was just some business deal. I could never talk about what had happened to my parents without getting all teary and tongue-tied. So I never did.

"Mom could have bought us our own place, but she wanted to live with her parents. Their house is huge. We have a whole floor all to ourselves. Plus a hot tub in the back. This place so needs a hot tub."

"When do you guys see your dad?"

"Oh, all the time. He comes to San Francisco on business, or we fly back to Boston at least once a month. We could have gone to Hawaii first class for free, we have so many miles. Mim made us donate them to this charity instead."

"That's kind of sweet that your dad and his mom are so close like that, though."

"Oh. I'm talking about my mom's mom. Dad's mom died a long time ago. He and Mim are close. It's like they're even closer since the divorce. I don't know why that is. Maybe because my mom's like out of the way. That makes it sound weird and creepy, but it isn't. Where do you guys live?"

"Connecticut. With our mother."

"She remarried?"

"No."

"Dating?"

"No. She says she doesn't want to put us kids through all that."

"All that what?"

"I don't know. Doesn't want to look slutty to us or something."

I'd managed not to think too much about Mom for the four days we'd been away. Picturing her in the house alone always got my stomach going. I imagined her sitting at the kitchen table, browsing through the morning paper as she drank her coffee. She hated when we left, though she tried to be brave about it, telling us all the things she was finally going to get to do around the house while we were out of the way. Like clean the closets and stuff. I was always worried that she was going to get depressed again.

"Maybe she does have a boyfriend—only he's married—so she can't let you meet him. Or maybe she's a lesbian, have you ever thought of that? And she's afraid you'll be grossed out—or embarrassed—or that they'll take her kids away like they did in Florida."

A secret romantic life sounded like a fun problem to have in a mom. Although she had gotten a lot better in the last year, my mom had been struggling with depression for a while and spent most of her time alone. I wasn't clear on what had happened to my parents' marriage, but the way she explained it, the depression had kept her from being a "good partner" to Dad, and their "bond had eroded."

There was no way to explain all this to Kelsey, so I let her go on with her imaginings. The lesbian thing shifted her attention away from my mother and back to her own life.

"We live next door to lesbians, and they have two kids. But where I live, that's normal."

Kelsey was the only reasonable friend material around, so I decided I could live with the overactive imagination. It might even be fun.

*   *   *

We sat next to each other at dinner. Chris was still freaked out by his run-in with the law. I think he was worried that Dad wasn't going to let him go camping with Dean's family at the end of the summer, so for once, he wasn't teasing me, making cracks under his breath about my eating and my weight.

"Hey Trace. How's it going?"

My brother never asked me how I was.

"Okay. How's it going with you?"

"Okay," he said, as his eyes wandered over to Kelsey. Our brother-sister moment was over as soon as it had begun.

Beka just sat there, listening to her Walkman, and Loraine tried her schoolteacher darnedest to get a conversation going with the new guests. She was talking to Kelsey and Josh, but she kept looking at Larry, who was talking out loud to no one in particular about the fabulous view out the dining room window, and wondering how long Sharon's family had owned Farnsworth House.

"I bet they bought it for a song."

"Well, not quite," answered Sharon, who had been stacking dinner plates on the sideboard. "It was expensive enough for the time. My grandfather was well off."

"Have you ever thought of turning it into a real hotel?" Larry asked, looking around the room. "With a few renovations, you could go four star."

"Oh, I'm well aware of the commercial potential

of this place," said Sharon with a nod and a little smile. Then, glancing over at the wall of pictures above the piano, she said, "But we're going to keep the Farnsworth family spirit alive as long as we can. The summer programs bring in enough to keep us going and maintain the house. I'm sure it's what my grandmother would have wanted."

During that first-day tour and history lesson, Sharon had told us all about how her grandfather had bought Farnsworth House in the 1920s from the original family that built it in the 1800s. He and his wife had hoped to have something like ten kids, but Sharon's mother was all they could come up with. They kept the big house anyway, and spent every summer there. But even a cook, a maid, a chauffeur, and a nanny couldn't fill up the place, and so Sharon's grandmother invited writers and artists to use the extra rooms. They got peace and quiet, a nice view of Nantucket Sound, and three meals a day while they wrote their books or painted their paintings or sculpted their statues. Some old paintings—by the ones who never got famous—still hung on the walls. The Farnsworths got "a house full of interesting people" in exchange for their support of the arts. Now Farnsworth House summer programs—Together Time, yoga and meditation, and artists' retreats—were Sharon's way of keeping up the family tradition.

Larry shrugged his shoulders and took one more look around. "Yeah well, that's a shame. You ever change your mind and need some backing . . ." He opened up his wallet, picked out a business card and held it out to Sharon.

"Thanks Larry. I'll put this back in the kitchen on our wall of cards."

Next to the industrial-sized refrigerator there was a huge bulletin board with tons of business cards tacked up, covering every last bit of cork. Some had little notes scrawled on them about how wonderful the food at Farnsworth House was, or about how relaxed people had felt on their yoga retreats and how much fun they'd had being with their kids. I didn't think that was what Larry had in mind when he whipped out his Wilcox Enterprises card.

"I'm just saying, you have no idea what you're sitting on here. You wouldn't have to sell out or anything. It would still be yours. You could keep it in the family."

"Really, Larry, I know what I'm doing." Something about the way Sharon said that—not bitchy or anything, just real thank-you-very-much firm—made Larry give up. She pushed her way through the swinging door that separated the dining room from the kitchen and for a moment, the whole table was quiet. Then, as the swinging door made its way back from the kitchen, it pushed a hot wave of smells back our way: fresh baked bread, steamy, hot corn on the cob, and barbecued something.

Larry went back to talking to no one in particular.

"Man what a gold mine she has here."

Loraine was still trying to get a group conversation going.

"Berkeley and Boston, talk about different worlds! What's that like, Kelsey, shuttling between California and New England?"

"What? Um. I don't know. It's warmer in the winter in Berkeley, though it rains a lot in winter. Some people don't know that. . . ."

Kelsey seemed to lose her train of thought when Paul walked in carrying a platter full of barbecued chicken. She stopped talking altogether as she watched him place it on the sideboard and head back to the kitchen. Everyone stared at the plate of sizzling meat, except Kelsey, whose eyes followed Paul.

When he was out of sight, she turned back to Loraine. "People think it's sunny all the time in California. Other than the weather, Berkeley and Cambridge aren't all that different. There's a Gap and a Starbucks near my house in Berkeley and in my dad's neighborhood in Cambridge. Sometimes, when I'm in the dressing room at Dad's Gap, I think I'm back in Berkeley. That's kind of weird."

"Yeah and they just opened a Trader Joe's in Boston," Josh chimed in. "So now we can have all the same foods on both coasts."

Paul walked back in with a big ceramic bowl full of steaming corncobs and Kelsey was lost again.

"Really?" said Loraine, still trying to get the table

engaged in a discussion. "I just read an article in the *Times* about how you find the same stores everywhere you go these days. You might have seen it Hank," she said, turning to my father, whose eyes were fixed on the corn. Everyone in our family loves corn on the cob.

When Paul returned from the kitchen for the final time, carrying Sharon's huge wooden salad bowl, no one even pretended to listen to Loraine anymore. Kelsey stared at Paul, Beka stared at Kelsey staring at Paul, and everyone else looked to Sharon for the okay to get up and fill our plates. She stood by the sideboard and gestured with open hands. "Tonight's dinner is barbecued chicken, fresh corn, green salad, and our renowned Farnsworth House rolls, made from my grandmother's original recipe." Before she could quite finish her nightly "Please, serve yourselves," we were all out of our seats and lined up at the sideboard.

Somehow, Kelsey managed to make it across the room, ignoring Beka's glare. She held her hand out to Paul, smiling. "I'm Kelsey."

He looked right at her instead of over her shoulder, which even though he's nice and all it always seems he does when he talks to me.

"Hi Kelsey, I'm Paul."

Beka bolted up from her chair, practically knocking it over, and turned to leave the table. Without even acknowledging Loraine's "Where are you going?" she made her way out of the dining room, across the parlor, and out the front door. We all heard the wood of the screen door bang as Loraine got up, and with a hurried, worried, and slightly annoyed "Excuse me," followed her daughter outside.

Sharon took over as conversation leader.

"This is the first corn we've had this season. Silver Queen. Got it at the farmer's market this morning." She looked over at my Dad, who was using part of a Farnsworth House roll to move the butter around his corn. "Well that's an interesting way to butter it."

"A little trick my ex-wife taught me."

What an ugly word, ex-wife. Especially when it's coming out of your own father's mouth. As soon as I heard him say it, I stopped buttering my corn and, while no one was looking my way, shoved the whole chunk of butter and the roll in my mouth. Chewing the creamy sweet mess, I no longer heard the voices in the room. I didn't have to think about my mother rattling around our empty house, or the bra in my father's hamper, or how I could never ever introduce myself to a cute guy the way Kelsey just had.

Chapter 4

Later, in the game room playing pool, I told Kelsey about Beka and Paul on the bed the night before.

"Do you think he really likes her? I mean, you don't even have to hear her talk to know she's a bitch. Nine ball. Corner pocket."

She spread herself out over the table, stretched her left arm out to steady her right, and shot. The yellow ball headed straight for the right pocket. Just as it clunked, someone said, "Aha, so the girl can play."

There, at the bottom of the steps stood the golden god of Farnsworth House.

Paul'd come downstairs every night so far, just after he and whoever had clean-up duty for the night finished the dishes. He kept his skateboards behind a couch next to the pool table. He'd grab one and head out to the school yard up the street where he and his friends passed the last minutes of daylight outdoing each other on their boards.

Emmy and I had gone the first night with our after-dinner Popsicles. I was supposed to be sort of babysitting, keeping her safe while she played on the equipment, or pushing her on a swing like I did at home. But all Emmy wanted to do was watch Paul and his friends skate. And so the two of us climbed to the top of the jungle gym and did just that.

The playground had a low, wide slide perfect for jumps. Plus there was this long handicapped ramp that went up to where the classrooms were. Paul and these two other guys would do these amazing jumps, sometimes twisting in the air before landing. They'd fall now and then, too, but they'd just laugh it off and start over. There were NO SKATEBOARDING signs on every wall, but no one paid attention. They all had "sk8R" spray painted across their boards, and talked in this funny Cape Cod skateboarding lingo, calling each other "dude" one second and "thou" or "thee" the next.

Every other night so far that week, Paul had barely grunted at me and the little kids before heading back up the stairs and out the door. Tonight, he walked over and stood right behind Kelsey as she spread herself over the table to take her next shot, which she blew.

"So, it was just luck," he said, daring her to defend herself.

She did. "No. It's just that I can't shoot when

there's someone breathing down my neck. She turned around and looked him right in the eye. "In fact, you're in violation of international pool rules there, buddy. Back off."

Kelsey was amazing. She was blushing—just slightly—but whatever she was feeling inside didn't keep her from knowing what to say and how to say it in a way that kept Paul interested.

"Okay, okay," said Paul, holding both hands up in surrender. "I'll keep my distance."

"That's right, keep your distance. Your turn, Tracy." She handed me the cue and coached me through my next shot, ignoring Paul.

I wish I could explain what Kelsey did. If I could explain it, then maybe I could someday do it myself. But I have never, not once in my life, been able to flirt. Her words said "go away." But something in the way she said it, in the way even that she turned away from him and toward me said, "not too far."

He stood there for a second more, without moving his eyes from her. Then he picked up his skateboard from behind the couch and headed out, taking one more look at Kelsey as he said, "Later," and bolted up the stairs.

Kelsey didn't face him when she said, "Later" back. Just kept on studying her next shot.

Looked like Beka was history.

When Emmy and Sammi and Sean piled down-stairs to rehearse the Munchkinland scene in their never-ending *Wizard of Oz* performance, Kelsey and I gave up on our game and escaped to the beach out front.

*   *   *

The sun was gone, though there was still a glow in the sky. An orange moon hung over Farnsworth House. There were lights on upstairs, and the parlor was lit up, too. Kelsey's dad was playing the piano, and Sharon was standing next to him, singing a song I recognized from one of my mom's old Beatles' albums. Loraine was lying back on the couch, and though I couldn't be sure, I thought I saw her lips moving, too. From here, Farnsworth House almost looked like the fun place Sharon wanted it to be, with spontaneous sing-alongs in the parlor and children playing in the game room. As long as you ignored the two teenagers—Chris and Beka, who I could just see out of the corner of my eye—smoking cigarettes down by the water.

It was a warm night, with a breeze coming off the sound. The air smelled salty. I used to love that smell when we were at our grandparents' cottage. Now it just made me feel funny.

"Well, he *is* cute," said Kelsey. "But I don't know. We're here for such a short time."

"Yeah, but he and Sharon live in Boston during the winter. He goes to school there."

"Really? Still, I don't know."

I just did not get Kelsey. She obviously liked Paul. But she wasn't going totally insane just because he seemed to like her, too. In fact, after he left the game room she had turned her attention back to our game, and focused on teaching me how to hit the balls without sending them bouncing across the table. "I'm not sure he's my type."

"Your type?"

"Yeah, my type. I went out with a skater for a year. That gets kind of old. Sometimes I'd be like, 'Hello C.J., remember me, your so-called girlfriend?' I didn't want to compete with a piece of wood on wheels, so I dumped him."

Two completely foreign concepts:

a.) Having a boyfriend.

b.) Dumping a boyfriend.

"Then there's Beka," I added.

"Oh. Now, I don't mind competing with her. Maybe I should go for him, just to save him from her clutches. Hey look, here comes your dad."

The screen door banged, and I looked up to see him and Loraine heading toward the beach. Loraine had a cigarette in one hand and a blanket in the other. Chris and Beka, who must have heard the door slam, too, disappeared down the beach.

"What does he see in her?" asked Kelsey. "She's all schoolteacher lectures and fake smiles. And cigarettes. Doesn't she know they make you stink?"

"Let's get out of here. I can't stand to watch." I started running down the beach toward the jetty. The breeze coming off the sound was turning into wind, and as I ran against it, my eyes teared up. By the time we reached the rocks, there were two obvious streams down my cheeks.

"Hey, hey. What's the matter?" Kelsey wrapped her long, tanned arms around my white shoulders as I nodded toward my father and Loraine.

"It's probably just one of those summer vacation things. It's not like she's going to end up your step-mother or anything. Wait! Oh. My. God. Wouldn't that be wild? You and Beka, stepsisters! What if you have to share a room and she brings guys in all the time?"

As if just the idea of me and Beka being stepsisters wasn't horrifying enough, Kelsey had to start imagining the adventures we'd have in our new blended family.

"Oh, oh. I know. You could get one of those baby monitors and hide it under her bed. Then put the other one next to her mother's side of her and your dad's bed."

Did she have to be so specific?

"All she has to do is invite one guy up there and boom! they'll send her away to an all-girl boarding school and you'll have your room to yourself again."

Whew. As much as I hated to picture certain of her scenarios, there was something fun about the way Kelsey's mind worked. She had this built-in sense of possibility. I'd only known her for a few hours, but

Farnsworth House felt like a different place. Maybe I would try to tell her a little more about why the Loraine thing upset me so much.

"And my mom. I know she misses him. I even hear them sometimes on the phone talking. They sound like they're still married. But she was the one who wanted the divorce. I don't get it."

Everyone tells me I'm lucky to have parents who are so "amicably" divorced, but to me that's what makes it so creepy. Dad comes in and has coffee with mom while he's waiting for us to get our coats and stuff. I've even heard them teasing each other. Sometimes I wish they would have a fight or something. My friend Zann's parents had fought over everything: who got the house, who got the kids, who got to take the kids skiing which weekends at the condo in Vermont. At one point her mother even hired a detective to find out if her father was hiding money from her.

I told Kelsey all about Mom's depression, about how at first it was mild, and they thought she could get through it with therapy and medication. But then there'd been those two weeks she had to stay in the hospital and Grandma had to come help Dad take care of us.

"Everyone in Berkeley's on antidepressants, according to my grandmother."

The flip side to Kelsey's sense of possibility: her trouble focusing.

"She's a therapist. Did I tell you that already? Her office is in the back yard. Sometimes if she has the window open I can hear her clients crying from upstairs in my room."

"That must be weird."

"Kind of. She's very popular. All day long, people come and go out of our back yard, sniffling and blowing their noses on their way back to their cars. I can see them just outside my window. She tells me it's a good thing that they're crying. It means they're facing their problems, 'feeling their feelings.'"

I didn't see what was so great about feeling your feelings. Mom's therapist convinced her to get us to see someone while they were splitting up. "It will be a chance to sort our your feelings," Mom said. The guy wanted us to call him Mike and bam, just like that tell him how it felt to have our dad move out.

"Bad." That's what I said. "It feels BAD, *Mike.*" Then I wouldn't say anything else. He tried all the tricks on me. Being my friend. Talking about school. But I wouldn't open my mouth. Finally, Mom said she wasn't going to pay if I wasn't going to talk, and she and I sat in the McDonald's across the street from Mike's office while Chris and Emmy had their sessions. I felt much better eating a large fries with lots of salt and ketchup than I did spending an hour in Mike's office.

"Here, call your mom."

Kelsey pulled out a bright green cell phone.

"Are you sure?"

"Go ahead. I've got like fifty-five minutes of free long distance left, and all my friends are at camp, where they're not allowed to use their phones."

"Actually, we're not supposed to use them here, either," I told her. Sharon makes everyone leave their cell phones with her when they come in the house. She says it 'gets in the way of being a family, which is what you came here for.'"

I could see what Sharon meant. My dad was pretty good about turning it off when he was with us, but sometimes, when there was an important meeting that he couldn't go to or something, he had someone call him to give him an update. He and Sharon worked out a deal where he could use it for an hour in the afternoon to answer all his messages and talk to his assistant. But he had to stand on the driveway.

I dialed. Seven rings and voice mail.

"Hi. Leave a message for Barbara, Chris, Tracy, or Emmy."

Now that was strange. Mom never went out. And she always answered the phone when we were away in case it was us calling.

Chapter 5

"Tracy. Wake up. Mom's on the phone."

Emmy was tugging my feet with one hand and holding a phone out with the other. She put the receiver on my pillow, and I groaned. Then I heard my mother's voice, from far away.

"Tracy, Tracy honey? Wake uh-up." She was kind of singing, like she used to do at home when I was little and had to get up for school. Before she got so sad, she'd sing whole songs to get us out of bed. She'd dance around the room, raising the blinds and singing corny stuff like, "Oh what a beautiful morning, oh what a beautiful day" in a big dramatic voice like the guy on the scratchy *Oklahoma* sound track she used to play on her old turntable. She hadn't done that in ages. Another family joke, gone to the divorced family graveyard.

Emmy had placed the phone upside down, and I was talking into the ear end and had the mouth end to my ear.

"Wait, wait, Mom." I fumbled with the cordless phone. "There. I'm here. Okay. Hi."

"Hi Sweetie, you having fun?"

"Yeah, I guess. There's a new family here, with a girl my age. Well, she's fifteen. But she's not all snotty about being older like the other one I told you about."

"That's great."

"I tried to call you last night. Where were you?"

"Oh, um, Joyce and I went out for coffee after our movie. Jenny's with her dad this weekend, so we decided to take advantage of our freedom."

"Oh. I thought Jenny was at Interlochen."

"Is that where she is? Oh, that's right. Well, we had fun, just the moms. So what are you guys doing today? Hitting the beach?"

"We're going on a field trip to the place where the Pilgrims landed."

"Plymouth? That's great. We went there before you kids were born, when we were visiting Grandma and Grandpa."

Normally, I would have been excited to go. I liked history and loved going to places where you could see how people lived in the olden days. But I wasn't so thrilled about going with the whole Farnsworth House gang.

The Plymouth trip was one of the official "excursions" that were part of the Together Time "experience." Maybe now that I had Kelsey it wouldn't be so bad. But I dreaded more time with Beka, and watching Loraine stalk my dad.

"Yeah, I guess. Hey, you should see the lady who runs this place. She's such a hippie, Mom. Tie dye, Birkenstocks, way long *gray* hair. Almost everything she wears is purple."

I didn't know why I was going on about Sharon. It was kind of like I thought maybe my mom could read my mind and know I was worried about Loraine and Dad, so I was changing the subject.

"Well, you know, some of our best friends are hippies, Tracy. Don't be too judgmental."

Maybe she was thinking about the picture that used to be by the side of her bed, of her and Dad when they were in college. They were both incredibly skinny, and both of them had on these really low hip-huggers. Plus they both had long, straight hair. At first you weren't even sure who was the boy and who was the girl, but then you looked closer and you could see a little bit of hair on his chin, and her two tiny bra-less breasts. They had explained to us that they were too young to be actual hippies, that they started college in 1974. "After the war was over," Dad would say. "But the party was still on," Mom would add. And then they would look at each other and laugh.

Once I asked my mom if they had done drugs, and

she admitted they'd "done some experimenting." And she explained that things were different then, too. "Not that I think this is really an excuse, honey, but everyone—I mean everyone, even our professors and some people's parents—not Grandma and Grandpa, don't worry—was experimenting." Plus she said, the pot they smoked was nothing like what's around today. "I know it sounds hypocritical to tell you I did it but you shouldn't, but that's what I'm doing. Now we know how dangerous it is. So please don't."

That was the extent of my "Say No to Drugs" talk. Which was enough, because I wasn't really interested. I had already done some "experimenting" of my own, sneaking gulps of vodka from the cabinet in Zann's kitchen, and aside from nearly gagging on the taste, I didn't like how it made me feel. I was pretty much a wimp in the substance abuse department. Well, except for snack foods.

I wasn't sure if it was just that I was half asleep, but Mom sounded funny. Almost happy. She changed the subject right away when I asked her about where she was last night. And that bit about Jenny being with her dad? Everyone knew that Jenny was going to Interlochen, the *"very selective"* music camp this summer to work on her cello playing. Her mother, Joyce, told us about it every chance she got: "They're giving her a scholarship, based on her audition. I am so proud." Mrs. Finch had wanted me to audition but dropped it when I started to slack off.

Anyway, Mom just sounded weird. I couldn't put my finger on it. What was I going to say, "What's wrong, Mom, you sound so happy?" I told her to say hi to Uncle Steve for me and to have fun antiquing with him and Roy.

"Oh, I will. You know those two." Roy and Steve shared a tiny apartment in Greenwich Village, with no room for anything but their futon, bookshelves, and stereo. They've been saying for years that they're going to get a country house, and they keep buying stuff and putting it in our attic and basement. Mom says they'd better do it soon, before she takes their stuff and starts her own antique store.

*   *   *

"Hey sleepy-butt," said Kelsey when I stumbled into the kitchen. "Want some cappuccino?" She was standing by the stove, watching one of those little hourglass-shaped espresso pots. Paul stood next to her, flipping French toast.

"I brought this from home. I've got to have my espresso every morning." As she said that, she snuck a look to see if Paul was listening. He didn't seem to be. Or maybe he was just pretending. I was so clueless when it came to the flirting thing.

"Umm, I think I'll have juice. Espresso's a little too much for me."

"Don't worry. My grandmother only lets me drink

decaf. Not that she'd ever know if I wanted to get the real stuff and switch it. But she's probably right. Once, when we had to study for a French final, my friend Amy and I stayed up all night, after having two full-strength double caps apiece."

"Did you pass?" asked Sharon, as she dipped a piece of bread into the egg mix and placed it on the griddle.

"Barely. Well, I got a seventy-eight. Amy got a ninety. I was so tired, I could hardly move my pen."

"*Ah bien. Combien du temps as-tu étudié le français?*" Sharon, long-haired hippie earth mother, suddenly sounded very sophisticated. Her accent was as good as my teacher's, Madame Granger, who was married to an actual French guy.

Kelsey was stumped. "Uh. *Pardon?*"

"I asked how long you've been studying."

"Oh. Just this one year."

"So you would say, '*J'étudie pendant une année.*'" She sounded just like the woman who did the tapes for our language lab.

Kelsey was starting to give me one of her eye rolls, when Paul started parlez-vousing.

"*Voulez-vous du pain perdu mademoiselle? Ou préférez-vous des ouefs ce matin?*"

You have to see a seventeen-year-old skateboarding American guy speaking perfect French to believe it. Kelsey just stood there, with her mouth and eyes wide open. I mean, Paul was so gorgeous, just standing there in front of the stove in his egg-stained cargo pants and Weezer T-shirt, spatula in hand. Any female person, except maybe his own mother, had to melt at the sight—and the sound.

"Umm. *Pardon?*" For the first time since she'd been at Farnsworth House, Kelsey was speechless.

"I said, would you like the French toast, *le pain perdu*, or the eggs this morning? In France, we eat bread, butter, and jam for breakfast. *C'est tout*. It's only you *Americaines*"—and he said this with a fake, exaggerated French accent, and fake exaggerated annoyance—"who insist on ziss silly con-coc-shee-un."

"Yeah, yeah. The crass Americans," said Sharon, like she'd heard all this before. "Give it a rest, or people might start to think you really are a snob." You could see though, that she wasn't really mad or anything. Actually, she looked kind of proud as she turned to us to explain.

"Paul's father is French. We lived in Paris when Paul was born and spent the first five years of his life there. Now he goes back once or twice a year to see Philippe. He'll be heading over when Together Time ends."

"Yeah. I can't wait. The skateboard scene in Paris is so cool. They've got all these parks and memorials, and as long as we don't get in anyone's way, the cops—*les flics*—don't bother us. It's not like here where they freak out if you use their precious playgrounds.

Merde." He flipped the four slices of egg-soaked bread in front of him.

"Someone called the cops again last night." He turned from the stove, puffed up his chest—obviously imitating someone—and continued, "'This is your last warning, guys. Read the sign: Violators will be prosecuted.' I mean, what kind of crap is that? You know Mom, I think I'm going to claim my French citizenship when I'm eighteen."

"Well, we always said it would be your decision, honey. I think those are done." She bent down to open the oven door, grabbed a pair of grungy oven mitts, and pulled out the large oval platter that had held last night's chicken. It was piled high with golden slices of the "silly concoction" I, for one, loved. Sharon held it while Paul placed the last four slices on top, and called out for all of Farnsworth House to hear: "*Venez! Venez! Venez a la salle à manger pour le petit déjeuner!*" and then, changing back into her American self, she half sang and half yelled, "Breakfast time, rise and shine, start your day off nice and fine."

Kelsey and I rolled our eyes at each other. How did this woman ever manage to produce such a cool son?

* * *

Since the trip to Plymouth was an official Together Time excursion, that meant:

a.) We were traveling in the old VW bus that Sharon and Paul had painted—purple of course—five years ago when they held the first Farnsworth House summer and,

b.) Paul was the official tour guide.

The bus only took eight passengers, so the other parents took our station wagon. Sharon drove, and Paul sat next to her. Sammi, Emmy, Sean, and Chris sat in the way back, and I sat in the middle between Kelsey and Beka, who had yet to say a word all morning.

As soon as we hit the highway, Sharon told Paul to "do the spiel."

He turned around, cleared his throat, and started. "Almost four hundred years ago . . ." He'd obviously told this story a lot. I tuned out until he mentioned that he and Sharon were descended from a Mayflower family, and the silent, sulking Beka came to life.

"Like the 'Mayflower Madam'? My mom went to college with her." Beka and Loraine always knew someone who knew someone who . . . You could tell she was hoping to impress Paul. I had no idea who she was talking about.

"That chick, man. She ruined it for us all." Paul shook his head and looked to Sharon for sympathy.

"Yeah. Now every time Paul tells guests about our pedigree, someone brings up Sidney Biddle Barrows."

"Who's Cindy Biddlebottoms?" asked Emmy from the back seat.

I was glad she asked. I wasn't going to parade my ignorance in front of Beka.

Sharon looked at Paul, who smiled and started to explain. "She's a, a . . ."

"A madam," said Beka.

"A madman?" asked Sean.

"She ran a dating service," said Sharon. I was beginning to get the picture. "This happened before any of you were born. She's a lady who got into trouble for selling something she wasn't supposed to be selling."

"Like drugs? Or guns?" asked Sean, hopefully.

"It's kind of a PG-13 story, guys," said Paul to the way-back crew. "Get back to me when you're thirteen and I'll tell you everything."

"She'll be long forgotten by the time you're running Farnsworth House, honey," Sharon assured him, with a little pat on his knee.

Without missing a beat, Kelsey Wilcox, expert flirt, was in there, getting Paul to talk about himself, just like all the articles on dating said to do. Only it didn't look like she was trying. It seemed totally spontaneous, like she really cared. Eyes wide and right on him, she asked, "You're gonna run Farnsworth House?"

"Well, it's been in the family for what, Mom? like almost a hundred years. . . ."

"Eighty," Sharon corrected him, holding up her pointer finger.

"Eighty's almost a hundred, Mom." Paul smiled, like this was some kind of inside joke.

Sharon smiled back and did this little sideways nod toward her son. "Yeah, you say that now."

"Okay." Paul turned back to us. "It's been in our family for eighty years, and now it's my mom's, and someday it's going to be mine, and she wants me to figure out some way to use it, some way to help people with it, like she does with the Together Times and the Artists' Escapes and the Meditation Retreats." He looked over at Sharon, who started in on the Farnsworth House history—again. Only this version had more personal details than I'd heard before.

"After Grandfather died, Grandmother couldn't bear to go to Farnsworth House without him, so she had it divided into apartments and kept the rent low— just enough, really, to keep the place up, to keep the roof repaired and the windows snug. But it wasn't the same without her, and the artists stopped coming. When I was a kid, there was the large downstairs apartment and the upstairs rooms were rented out to college boys working summer jobs. That explains a lot about the condition of those rooms up there, by the way."

I thought about the graffiti I'd found carved into the sloping ceiling above my bed: "Caroline," and "J.A.S., Harvard '58." There was one that said "S.F.H."

"My grandmother left me the house, hoping it would give me a reason to settle down. But I was living in Paris with Philippe then, and Massachusetts seemed so, you know, American and boring. So I just let things continue as they had. When Philippe's work wasn't selling, we moved over here, where we could live for free. But he couldn't stand to be away from Paris. So he left, and we stayed." She brushed Paul's upper arm for a moment, glancing at him briefly and then turning her eyes back on the road.

"Boy was that a lonely winter. But one day, I was looking through some of my grandmother's old photos of Farnsworth House in the twenties. The parlor was full of writers and musicians. People were dancing or standing around the piano singing. Right then and there, I decided to fill up Farnsworth House again. But I'd update the mission. Expand a little. Here I was, thirty years old, a single mother, all alone. Poor Paul didn't have anyone to play with. So the first thing I did was start Together Time."

Without missing a beat, Paul said, "Yeah, and now I have lots of people to play with."

On either side of me, Kelsey and Beka each squirmed.

✳Chapter 6✳

"Now that's a million dollar view!"

Even though it was an obnoxious way to put it, I could see what Larry meant.

Plymouth—or Plimoth, as it's officially called because that's how they spelled it back when spelling was a less exact science—is amazing. First of all, it's right on the water. They've re-created the village exactly as it stood in 1627, after the Pilgrims had been here a few years, with a little dirt street and these thatch-roofed cottages that are half underground. Your eyes follow the road and it seems to drop off into the big old Atlantic Ocean.

"I could get half a million apiece for one-bedroom condos here. Up to a million for two beds and two baths. With golf and tennis? I could retire, send my kids—and all of your kids—through college. I'd call it 'The Landing, Cape Cod's Most Exclusive Resort,'" Larry said, sweeping his hand across an imaginary billboard in the cloudless July sky.

Loraine looked horrified. "Sure Larry, maybe you can get them to sell you the dunes outside Provincetown while you're at it. Make that a gated community, too. Who needs the National Seashore after all? We'll all just go to Jones Beach on the weekends while you and your rich friends enjoy yourselves in peace and quiet."

Kelsey jumped to her father's defense. "He always does this, Loraine. He can't help but see real estate wherever he goes. When we went to the Grand Canyon he talked about putting in a spa at the bottom. It's just talk."

"Thanks for defending your old dad, honey." Larry put his arm around her.

Sharon hadn't come back from parking the bus yet. Seeing an opportunity, Loraine took charge.

"Okay, one two three four adults, five 'youths twelve to seventeen,' and four kids," she said to the woman at the desk, who was decked out in full Pilgrim wear: a black-and-white bonnet/kerchief thing tied under her chin, a white collar over a drab, dark gray dress. I couldn't help but think she was probably pretty hot under all that. And I wondered if she was allowed to wear normal, modern-day underwear. "What do we owe you? Larry, maybe you should get this. You know, give a little back to the community."

With a "why not?" shrug, Larry dug into his shorts pocket for his wallet. But before he could pull out any money, Sharon ran up, panting slightly from her walk up the hill.

"No, no. Excursions are included in the price of your stay." She stepped in front of Larry. "Hi Gladys. We're prepaid."

"Sharon! Hi. I didn't realize they were yours. Go right in, folks." As each of us filed past her, she said "Welcome to Plimoth Plantation," and handed us a brochure. Once we were all past the gate, she gave us a little introductory talk, explaining that the "costumed interpretive guides" were there to teach us about everyday life in the sixteen hundreds. "Don't hesitate to ask anything. Remember, the only stupid question is the one you don't ask."

Kelsey and I asked if we could walk around by ourselves, which prompted a parental huddle. Heads nodded and looked our way, then returned to the huddle and whispered some more. Finally, they broke, giving all the fourteen-and-over kids permission to explore on our own, as long as we checked in at lunchtime.

* * *

I liked seeing the small houses, imagining life four hundred years before. No electricity, no plumbing.

Nothing to read but the Bible. If I lived back then, I wouldn't be sneaking Ding Dongs and M&M's in the middle of the night. Salt-cured fish and dried cranberries hardly seemed worth the trouble. So I was pretty sure I'd be a thin Pilgrim. And I was pretty sure my parents wouldn't have gotten divorced. They wouldn't have been allowed to unless one of them committed adultery, and then they might hang for the offense. Under those rules, they probably would have figured out a way to make their marriage work.

But I wasn't sure my mom would have been any happier. We heard about this one Pilgrim woman who went insane as soon as the boats landed on Cape Cod. The endless trees and sand were so depressing, she drowned herself in that big old Atlantic.

"What did the Pilgrims eat for dinner?" I asked this one guy with the thickest beard I'd ever seen.

"My goodwife Sarah and Goody Browne are garbaging the chicken yonder," he said, which I gathered meant that his wife and her friend were plucking and cleaning the guts out of a chicken. On the way out of that house we saw a bloodstained tree stump with feathers scattered around it. An ax was stuck in the center.

In the forge, the blacksmith's shop, we found three grimy guys making nails. The oldest one, who also had one of those big, scraggly beards, was the blacksmith. The two younger guys, with barely a chin's worth of facial hair between them, were the apprentices. Every inch of every one of them was covered in grime. Their hands were black with soot, their puffy, once-white shirts were torn and streaked with dirt, and their faces were so greasy they shone. And yet, hard as it might be to believe, I thought they were kind of cute. One was tall and lanky with brown curly hair that went over his ears, and the other was a little shorter and wider. Not fat or anything, just kind of wide compared with the other guy. His hair was dark brown, almost black, and straight, and he wore it back in a ponytail tied with a piece of leather.

I had this weird feeling that I'd seen them before, but I figured you'd seen one grimy blacksmith, you'd seen them all. It must have been a movie or something.

Kelsey poked her elbow into my side, which I took to mean something like, "Are you seeing what I'm seeing?"

I elbowed "Yeah, I am" back.

We stood watching as they heated little bits of metal over an open flame, then banged them into shape against an anvil. Half-moons of sweat had formed under their armpits, and they kept using their puffy sleeves to wipe the sweat dripping down their foreheads and off their noses. Kelsey and I elbowed back and forth all the while.

Finally, Kelsey spoke. "Excuse me, excuse me. I

don't want to be rude, but don't you guys ever take baths?" I thought this was pushing the stupid question thing a little. They looked at her, then at each other, and smiled in a way that looked like they'd heard this question before.

"I mean, you're Puritans, right? Aren't there rules about hygiene?"

The tall one answered her, talking in an accent so thick it made English sound like a foreign language.

"Ah, methinks I understand the question. M'lady, 'tis not ourselves use this word 'Puritan,' to speak of ourselves. No, no. Rather, those who would disparage our piety call us by that term, those who persecuted us back in England. No. We call ourselves mere Christians. As for our besmirched appearance, well—" Here he stopped to look at his hands, the soil on his white puffy sleeves. "We believe the work we do honors our Lord in Heaven much more than external cleanliness."

The dark-haired apprentice added, "We bathe but one or two times a year. 'Tis a dangerous thing, immersing thy limbs in water." As he turned his attention back to the nail on the anvil, I thought I saw a trace of a smile. But it disappeared just as quickly as it had appeared.

"But didn't they—I mean, don't you—didn't they . . ." Kelsey was stumped. Meeting two guys our own age dressed like Pilgrims and speaking so formally had her totally tongue-tied.

This encounter gave me a chance to study Kelsey's technique, which I realized wasn't a technique at all. Her flirtatiousness wasn't self-conscious. She was just friendly and outgoing; curious and confident. And she liked guys. She didn't seem to be thinking about every word that came out of her mouth, wondering what the guys would think of her.

"Don't you get tired of going around like that?" she said, motioning with her head at their disgusting clothes.

What the tall apprentice said next was so intense, it was hard to tell if he was acting. "Let others such as yourselves adorn themselves in fine fabrics, in sensuous perfumes."

Then he gave Kelsey, who was wearing a very short, bright green sundress, with three-inch green-and-yellow flip-flops, who had rubbed a little glitter lotion on her tanned shoulders that morning, a dramatic, head-to-toe inspection. Pointing at her accusingly, he said, "Oh, yes. Your countenances appear unblemished, your garments fine. But what is on the inside? Hmm? On the soul." And with that, he held a fist to his chest and stared into her eyes. Then he turned away from her abruptly, picked up another future nail with his tongs and held it over the open flame. His movements and manner said, "I've had enough of you."

Personally, I thought the guy was flirting, but Kelsey totally freaked, and she flip-flopped her way out as fast as she could, pulling me by my elbow. "Let's get out of here."

*   *   *

As soon as we had escaped the heat of the black-smiths, we caught up with Sharon and Paul, who were on their way to "Hobbamock's Homestead," the Native American part of town, which Sharon said was her favorite. Loraine and Larry, who had the little kids, found us there. Chris and Beka and my dad were off watching the video presentation in the air-conditioned auditorium.

Hobbamock's Homestead was pretty cool. Very back-to-nature, with mats woven out of reeds and fabrics made with vegetable dyes. I could see why Sharon would like it so much.

Larry started elaborating on his plans for "The Landing," saying he'd build a modern sauna and steam room that looked like a wigwam on the outside, next to a big swimming pool that would be painted to look like a spring-fed pond. Loraine looked like she wanted to punch him, until he said he'd dress the life-guards in native clothing and it dawned on her that he was kidding.

A wigwam labeled "the menstrual hut" prompted a little debate between Sharon and Loraine.

"You know, I've sometimes thought I should build a little menstrual hut in the back yard of Farnsworth

House. Lots of fluffy pillows and a big claw-foot tub. When it was your time, you'd just go to the hut and rest. I'd fill it with great, comforting books and we'd have a complete library of weepy chick flicks. I'd hire Paul and his friends to cook meals and leave them outside the door."

Of course, Loraine had to disagree. "But it's so sexist. Like those people who say we can never have a woman president, just because there's this little hormonal event once a month. Menstruation isn't a disability, Sharon."

"I'm not saying it is. I'm just saying the Wampanoags might have had a good idea when they gave menstruating women a place apart, a place to go and enjoy the miracle of it all."

Now I was the one grabbing Kelsey by the elbow.

"Let's get out of here," I whispered. I couldn't stand to be in the same room with my brother or any male when a Tampax or Stayfree commercial came on. Now here were Sharon and Loraine debating the merits of a menstrual hut in front of the fathers *and* Paul *and* anyone else who might be walking by.

"What? Oh, okay." Kelsey wasn't the least bit embarrassed. As we made our way toward the snack bar she explained. "We talk about stuff like that at our house all the time. When I got my period, Mim took me out for a 'Welcome to Womanhood' dinner at Chez Panisse—that's this really famous restaurant in Berkeley. The waiter had been one of her clients and she told him what we were celebrating. I thought I would die of embarrassment, but then he brought me this tiny glass of champagne and a platter with chocolate mousse, crème brûlée, and lemon tart on the house, and I got over it."

*　*　*

The snack bar at the visitor's center was full of tourists like us. Families in their Cape Cod T-shirts stuffing down hot dogs and hamburgers. An old woman reading out loud from her guidebook: "It says here that the cows come from Ireland. How about that Georgie, the Irish have been here from the beginning."

Old Georgie just kind of grunted back, more interested in his clam chowder than his wife's efforts to educate him.

We found an empty table toward the back of the picnic area, near where some of the interpretive guides were sitting in their costumes. I thought it was kind of weird that they didn't make them eat somewhere else. Seeing them now, stuffing their faces with the same food we were eating, speaking normal English, kind of broke the spell. No sign of the two guys who'd spooked us at the forge.

After eating our peanut butter and jelly on whole wheat and picking all the M&M's out of our trail mix, Kelsey and I got up to buy ice-cream cones at the counter. When we returned to our table, we spied our grimy friends, sitting in the middle of the guides' table.

They'd wiped their faces clean, but still sat in the same dirty clothes. Each had a wide-brimmed leather hat sitting before him on the table. The shorter one noticed us first, and then nudged the other, who turned around and gave Kelsey that same once-over glance I'd seen before.

"Well, well, if it isn't m'lady."

Out here in the real world, I guess Kelsey didn't find him as intimidating, and she fell naturally into her flirtatious mode.

"Sir, I'm not your lady."

"You're already spoken for, then?"

"I'm nobody's lady, thank you very much. You know, a lot's happened in four hundred years. Women are more independent than they were in your time."

Without thinking, I jumped into the fray. "Yeah. And we don't wear scarlet letters anymore either. We don't apologize for who we are."

It was the weirdest thing. Without thinking, inspired by my new expert flirt friend, I spoke my first flirtatious words. And it worked. I mean, I can't really say "it worked" because that would make it sound like I was trying to do something when I wasn't trying to do anything. I just got caught up in the moment, and before I knew it, the other guy stood up, walked toward our table, swung his leg over the bench and sat down directly in front of me, hot dog in hand.

"So, who are you?"

Ah, that simple and yet not-so-simple question.

"Um, Tracy. I'm Tracy Forrester." And just as I said that, Kelsey abandoned me, flip-flopping over to give the other blacksmith a few more pieces of her California mind. I was staring at her back, hoping she'd feel my pain and turn around, when I heard, "Hello Tracy Forrester. I'm Kevin, Kevin Kincaid. I'm sixteen, and I'm going to be an actor. This is my first gig." He took one last bite of his hot dog, a sip of his Coke, and sat there, chewing.

I couldn't think of a thing to say back.

He chewed that last bite for what seemed like a very long time, just looking at me, holding up his finger. Then, after finally gulping, he wiped his mouth with that disgusting sleeve of his and said, "How about you?"

"How about me?"

"Yeah, what are your plans?"

"Um, well, my immediate plans are to eat this ice-cream cone. And later today I thought I might go swimming back at Farnsworth House if it's warm enough."

It made total sense that he was a drama nerd. If we had a place like Plimoth in my town, I'm sure all of Jackson High's drama nerds would be working there. Drama nerds lived in a world of their own. Not total geeks, yet not popular either. But the thing was, they didn't care. They dressed only to impress each other. Some of the guys wore eyeliner. The girls might dress punky one day and slutty the next, then show up in sweats and a T-shirt when they weren't in the mood to be someone else. Caitlin, my old best friend, hung out with them ever since she was in the chorus of *Oliver* the summer after eighth grade. She saw *Rent* something like thirty times.

"So, you're staying at Paul's mom's place?"

"What? Yeah, how'd you know?"

"Well, Tracy, you did just tell me that you were going swimming at Farnsworth House." It was amazing how a simple conversation with a *kinda* cute guy could destroy your otherwise pretty strong thinking skills. "I know Paul. And I saw you the other night."

"You saw me?"

"Yeah. On the playground. You and your little sister were sitting on the jungle gym eating Popsicles while we were skating."

The thought of someone noticing me took me entirely by surprise.

"Where is she?"

"Who?"

"Little sister."

"Oh. She's got someone her own age to hang out with now. I think they're over at the gift shop with the parents."

"And you've got someone your own age to hang

out with, too." He turned back to look at Kelsey and the other guy, who, judging by the way their heads were inclining toward each other over the picnic table, had gotten past the hostility. "Excuse me, excuse me, ahem." I couldn't tell if Kevin was switching back into his Pilgrim persona to get rid of me or impress me. "Goodman, methinks 'tis time we end this most pleasant interlude and return to God's work."

"Goodman" looked up and waved. "Aye, aye good-fellow, just one moment more, please." He said that in his booming, theater voice, then dropped his head and voice to ask Kelsey something.

Kelsey wasn't so good at whispering. "We're not supposed to use our cell phones at Farnsworth House. But maybe if we set up a time, I can wait outside or something." She fished around in her little green purse and found a scrap of paper and a bright green pen. She scribbled her number and handed it to the blacksmith, who, lacking pockets, stashed it under the cuff of his puffy sleeve.

"Well, maybe I'll see you around." When Kevin said that, I thought for sure he was blowing me off. But then, as he grabbed his leather hat and stood up to go, he turned back and looked right into my eyes. "Adieu, sweet lass, adieu. Perhaps we will meet on the morrow."

* * *

Sometimes I wish you could borrow personality traits. I would have given anything to have had the use of Kelsey's social skills for just that split second. Surely I would have been able to come up with something more than "yeah," and "um," and, "maybe" in response.

Chapter 7

The ride back was quiet. We'd lost the warm and fuzzy almost-like-a-family feeling we'd had on the way there. It looked like Beka'd decided to forget Paul, or to pretend to forget him, and she and Chris were in the way back, plugged into the Walkman again. Kelsey was staring off into the pine trees that lined the highway, thinking, no doubt, about Dave the blacksmith, who was going to call her at four forty-five that afternoon. She had her hand in her purse, and I just knew she was holding her contraband Nokia. Every once in a while I'd see her glance at the clock on the dashboard.

I spent most of the car ride memorizing the information in the Plimoth Plantation brochure, preparing myself in case I ever did see Kevin again. At least then I'd have some conversation material.

How did they do it? The Kevins and Kelseys and

Daves of the world? How did they just meet a person and get going like that? Why couldn't I? My parents said I talked "early and often," that once I got the hang of it, I didn't seem to stop. We had a box of cassettes back home with my two-year-old voice telling long, involved stories about my stuffed animals.

Now, at fourteen, talking to a guy felt like trying to climb a mountain with a sixty-pound pack on my back. And weights around my ankles.

* * *

As we pulled into the driveway, I tried to figure out how I could get away from everyone for a little while. I loved hanging with Kelsey, but I knew she'd want to talk about Kevin and Dave, and I wasn't ready for that. I needed time alone.

Then Sharon reminded me that I was scheduled for dinner prep duty. "We've got lots of potatoes to peel."

Guest participation in cooking and cleanup was supposed to add to the "family feeling" at Farnsworth House. Yeah, the family feeling of claustrophobia, I thought at first. But then I'd had cleanup duty the first night, and it wasn't as bad as I'd imagined. I could see what she meant. Today though, sitting in the kitchen with her and Paul after our trip to Plymouth and my so-called conversation with Kevin wasn't my first choice of activity.

First choice would have been to get my hands on a

package of Oreos and a carton of milk and find a quiet place to stuff myself in peace. There is nothing like that sweet, crunchy mush that milk and Oreos make in your mouth to take your mind off things.

But it was my turn, and it was too late to trade with anyone, so instead of downing Oreos I was peeling organic russet potatoes. Five pounds of them, with Sharon and Paul, who were making yet another Farnsworth House specialty, homemade french fries for the steak-frites dinner.

Food was the one area where Sharon broke out of the hippie mold. When we first arrived, I expected chickpea casseroles and tempeh burgers, with Rice Dream instead of ice cream for dessert. I guess it was all that time she spent in France.

Sharon spread a newspaper out over the big round table at the back of the kitchen and handed Paul and me each a peeler. "You know how to use one of these, Tracy?"

"Yeah. We usually just get frozen french fries at home. But I've peeled carrots." There'd been a time a few months back when I'd tried to diet. I lasted about five days eating nothing but carrots or apples in between meals. Mom tried to help me by cooking low-fat recipes and taking walks with me after dinner. But then she fell into one of her moods and I found myself up to my old tricks late at night.

I picked up one of the big brown potatoes out of the sack and started to peel.

"You didn't tell me Kevin and Dave were working at Plymouth this summer," Sharon said to Paul. My potato, which was half naked at this point, slipped out of my hands, and bounced off of the underside of Paul's arm.

"Whoa. Watch it there, these taters can hurt someone. Here, let me show you."

As with almost everything he did, Paul had a technique for potato peeling. Holding just the top, he balanced the bottom against the table. Then, in seconds, he peeled from top to bottom, letting the thin slivers of skin form a neat pile below. He'd inspect for spots, dig them out with the tip of the peeler, and then toss the fleshy white thing into the soup pot in the middle of the table.

"See? Always point away. Otherwise you might hurt someone. Look here."

He offered the inside of his arm and pointed to a tiny half-moon scar just below his elbow.

"Go ahead, feel it." He kept the arm extended and lifted up slightly.

It was just an arm, right? It shouldn't have been such a big deal. But I swear it must have taken me thirty seconds to extend my finger out so that I could touch the smooth, hard spot.

"That's how I finally learned to peel potatoes safely. Summer of ninety-eight. Man was that a messy night. No stitches, though. The cut wasn't clean enough. That's it, you got it."

Hoping they wouldn't notice my blushing, I'd picked up a new potato and started peeling vigorously. Just when my heartbeat and blood pressure had almost recovered from touching the fleshy inside of Paul's arm, the subject of Kevin came up again.

"Yeah. They auditioned at the end of last month. I wouldn't have wanted to be around if they didn't get it," said Paul. "Man, those guys drove me nuts with the thee's and thou's when we were skating. 'Get thee out of harm's way,' before nailing a hammer. 'Dost thou this, mind thy that' when they were supposed to be helping me build a jump. For one week, they refused to speak normal English. Said they had to stay 'in character.'"

"Well, it's nice to see that kind of enthusiasm."

"Kevin thinks he's going to be famous."

"You never know. You met Kevin today, Tracy, didn't you?"

Leave it to Sharon to try to include me in the conversation. "Um, yeah. Kelsey and I met him and Dave at the blacksmith shop." I tried to make it sound casual.

"Kevin's a nice kid. Remember that summer I taught you guys to cook?"

"Yeah, Mom. How could I forget? Hey, you missed a spot here." Paul tossed what I hoped would be my last potato back. I dug out the offending brown stuff and handed it back to him for inspection. "Cool. They have to be perfect before they can earn the honor of being fried in our fat. You haven't tasted french fries until

you've tasted Farnsworth Frites. The secret's in the fat."
As he said this, he stepped over to the industrial size
refrigerator and rummaged around on the bottom shelf
for a while before pulling out a big, unmarked can with
a plastic top.

Loraine walked into the kitchen just in time to see
Paul scoop lard into the pan on the stove. Her face
turned white.

"You're not actually going to cook with that stuff,
are you?" she gasped.

Paul looked at Sharon, who answered for him.

"It's the only way, Loraine."

"What about canola oil or safflower?"

"We've tried the healthy route. There's no crunch,
and they don't turn brown. Lard's the only way."

"Well, I just hope there's a big salad tonight,"
Loraine said as she grabbed a glass from the cabinet
and poured herself some water from the filtered spigot
at the sink before turning to walk into the dining room.

Loraine's scene made Sharon and Paul forget all
about Kevin for the moment.

Not me.

Chapter 8

"Well, maybe I'll just have a few," Loraine said as she lifted exactly four of the golden fries with the tongs and placed them on her plate.

They were so good, so thin and crispy and perfectly salted, that even Loraine, the most determined fat resister I'd ever met, could not say no.

Something weird happened to me that night. Before dinner, I'd been fantasizing about throwing myself into a bag of Oreos, but kitchen duty had kept me from that. Then, as I worked on the meal with Sharon and Paul, I was so absorbed in the conversation and activity, I almost forgot about eating. When we finally sat down to enjoy what we'd made, I didn't feel the need to stuff myself. I took a big serving of fries on my plate, worried that by the time I wanted seconds they'd be gone, but I only got halfway through. I enjoyed every bite, especially the fries that had soaked up the juice from the meat. But for the first time in a very long while, I stopped eating before my plate was empty.

"Careful there Loraine, I think I see some fat emerging on your upper right arm." If I hadn't known that Larry was engaged, I would have thought he was interested in Loraine by the way he kept teasing her.

"Oh. Come on. Can't a person be concerned about her health? Really, it's not so much about looks for me. There's been a lot of heart disease in my family." She finished the last of the four fries she had allotted herself and eyed the platter on the sideboard, then realized everyone was eyeing her.

"I know, I know. I'm down to ten a day now, which is half of what I used to smoke. In another month I'm going to five, and then, come September, when school starts it's cold turkey."

"You've said that before, Mom." There was a tone in Beka's voice that seemed more real than almost anything I'd heard her say all summer.

I was almost feeling sorry for Loraine and Beka, when Kelsey turned to me and whispered, "Kevin and Dave want us to meet them up at the playground after dinner."

Even though I was pretty sure that most of the wanting was on Dave's part, directed toward Kelsey, I couldn't help but feel a little jump in my stomach when I heard her say "Kevin" and thought about seeing him again so soon.

"Yeah. I've got dish duty, though," she said, glancing up at the Together Time Chore Chart on the wall by the door to the kitchen. Her name was up there next to "Kitchen Detail Evening Cleanup (K.P./P.M.)," along with Loraine's and Larry's.

"I'll help you," I said. "It'll go faster that way."

We were having make-your-own strawberry short-cake for dessert, and I piled my bowl high with vanilla ice cream and the fresh, sugar-sprinkled berries that Sharon and I had hulled. But when I sat down again, I found I could only manage three or four bites. The thought of seeing Kevin again so soon made me lose my appetite. I wasn't sure what I expected to happen up at the school yard, but I wanted to get there as soon as we could.

*   *   *

"Sit still. Your feet say a lot about who you are."

We'd blazed through the dishes in record time, scraping, rinsing, and stacking them in Sharon's restaurant-style dishwasher before everyone else was finished with dessert. Larry and Loraine said they'd do the rest.

I wanted to leave right away, but Kelsey insisted on giving me a quick pedicure. I hadn't had my toenails painted since I was like seven and my mom would sometimes dab some polish on mine when she did her own. My feet had always been the most ticklish part of me. I had to take long, deep breaths to keep from cracking up and pulling them back while Kelsey was working on me.

"This really ought to be done by a professional, but there's no time for that. Luckily, I brought my magic drying stuff." She took out a can of something that looked like spray paint and shook it before covering her mouth and spraying a clear coat over the shimmery blue polish she'd just slapped on.

"There. Now, you've got to wear these." Kelsey reached under her bed and pulled out a pair of her signature chunky flip-flops: pink and yellow, with a shimmery blue flower in the middle.

I looked down at my so-so feet. They weren't ugly or anything. None of my toes was a weird size. We used to have this babysitter, Mary Beth, whose middle toe was freakishly longer than the rest of her toes. Chris said it made it look like her feet were giving you the finger, which was pretty funny, because Mary Beth was probably the biggest prude in our whole town, who would never give anyone the finger no matter how mad she was. She was in high school when she sat for us, but she looked like a cross between a grown woman and a little girl, always in buttoned-up blouses and big baggy khakis. I figured it had something to do with the fact that she had been home schooled until ninth grade, when she enrolled in Jackson so she could take AP classes.

Mary Beth was a great babysitter. You couldn't ask for anyone nicer. But you could tell that she had kind of missed out on stuff by spending all those years at home without any peers to pressure her into experimenting a little with her looks.

I wasn't sure if, in this case, Kelsey's peer pressure was doing me any good. The toes and the flip-flops looked fine on their own. But they really didn't go with the rest of me.

My style was somewhere between Mary Beth's plainness and Kelsey's flashiness. I was probably closer to Mary Beth than Kelsey, but not completely out of it or anything. I liked loose pants, mostly because my butt and thighs changed size a lot, depending on how much eating I was doing, and I didn't want to take a chance on things getting too tight. On top I mostly wore T-shirts. I had a whole collection of Brett Smiths, one for each CD and tour. Most of them I'd bought over the Internet or at record stores, except the one I put on for our walk to the playground, "Last Night at the Lake," which my uncle Steve bought for me at the concert we'd gone to for my birthday in March.

I wore it with the army pants I'd inherited from my mom's trunk full of old college clothes. They were supposed to be Italian or something, made from this really thick, olive-green cotton, and between my mother's wearing them through college and the year or so since she'd handed them on to me, they had been washed so many times that they were incredibly soft and comfortable. Just the right size, too. A little snug around the waist, but lots of room in the legs. The T-shirt went with them perfectly, because the design, which showed Brett sitting on a dock under a starry sky, had this green border around it that matched the pants perfectly, without looking too outfit-y.

I am not an outfit girl.

Kelsey was a total outfit girl. She rummaged through her stuff to find an orange miniskirt and yellow tank top. When she had squeezed herself into them and rubbed a little glitter lotion on her shoulders, she looked me up and down and said, "Maybe you should wear your leather sandals."

She was right. The bright rubber things did not go with the shirt and pants I had on at all, and I was relieved to be able to wear my flat, leather-strapped sandals. I get a new pair every summer, from this little store in our town that sells leather things from all over the world. If you wear them enough, they kind of shape themselves to your feet.

Wearing Kelsey's rubber flip-flops felt a bit like trying to walk in scuba-diving flippers, something I had done one year for Halloween, when I fell and scraped up my knee pretty badly, so I was relieved to be granted permission to be myself.

Of course, being myself was also a problem. I had no idea how to proceed with the evening. I mean, I knew how to walk, so I was pretty sure I could get up to the playground. But I didn't know what I would do once we were there.

I looked at Kelsey, all shimmery and shiny and well—sexy—in her skirt and top. There was nothing in her expression that indicated the least amount of fear or uncertainty about who she was or what she was doing. "Let's go," she said as she turned toward the door that led to the back stairs.

I took a deep breath and followed.

Chapter 9

As we approached the playground, we heard the clatter of skateboards landing, the crackly roll of the wheels on concrete, and those booming theater voices.

"Whoa. Be ye careful, dear sir."

"Fie! Fie! A pox on both your houses!"

I wasn't sure how much of their talk was authentically Pilgrim, but it was funny.

We entered through a gate below the ramp they used for their jumps. They were standing at the top, right before the blue person-in-a-wheelchair handicapped access sign and another that said NO SKATEBOARDING. VIOLATORS WILL BE PROSECUTED TO THE FULL EXTENT OF THE LAW. MAXIMUM FINE $500, BARNSTABLE COUNTY ORDINANCE # 32.14.10.

As soon as the guys saw us, they hopped on their boards and rolled down the ramp and out over a plank of wood that led to a three-foot drop. Dave went first, wobbling a bit on landing, but then recovering. Then Kevin made a clean jump. After rolling a little farther down the asphalt, he did this little circle thing and then came to a complete stop facing me and Kelsey.

She scoffed. "If they think they're going to impress us with their skateboarding skills, they are so wrong."

I was impressed. Very impressed. Kevin's hair was still in a ponytail, and he wore a UMass lacrosse cap. I watched as he made the slightest moves with his hips and knees to steer himself around.

"Good evening, fair wenches," said Dave, rolling toward us. I wasn't an expert, but I was pretty sure he had ventured off the list of approved vocabulary words for the Plimoth Plantation interpretive guides. He lifted his baseball cap off his head while he was still moving. Then he jumped off his board, landed right in front of Kelsey, and bowed. She let out the tiniest little sound, kind of like a giggle, kind of like a cough. Whatever it was, I was glad to hear it. If she had been able to resist that move, then I'd have to conclude that she wasn't human.

Kevin rolled up behind him and just said, "Hey." A few small drops of sweat had gathered above his lip, where I noticed a trace of dark stubble that hadn't been there that afternoon. There was another patch on the end of his chin and one on each cheek as well.

"Hey," was all I could manage back.

Kelsey and Dave started out in full flirt mode. She grabbed his board, kicked off her platform flip-flops, and showed him that she could pretty much do all the moves he had been doing a moment before.

Kevin pointed to my shirt and said, "Cool CD."

Now this was a first. I had never met a male Brett Smith fan. I wondered for a second if he might just be saying that to be nice, but then he started to sing "Last Night at the Lake":

So dark I can't see
Can't see where the sky ends
Can't see where the water begins,

Don't know where you start
Don't know where I end
Don't know whose heart is beating now

And I can't find
The border between us,
Can't find the line, can't find the line.

He had Brett's inflections just right, and he closed his eyes while he sang. It looked real and it sounded good.

"Wow. Most guys won't admit to liking Brett, even when they do."

"Yeah, well, when your sister plays her nonstop, you can't help but listen. And if you listen, you can't help but notice that she's like one of the most talented singer-songwriters around today. I can pick a few of her songs out on my guitar. You play anything?"

"Piano. Or, well, used to."

"Why'd you stop?"

"Oh, you know, it got to be a pain to keep up. Too much to do." I thought of the last lesson Dad had taken me to. He was so late we had to skip the bagel stop and barely made it to Mrs. Finch's on time. "And there was other stuff I wanted to do."

So far, my Saturday mornings had been a little aimless since giving up the piano, but I was planning to get back to writing poems and studying for the SATs. I had gotten as far as buying a book for that. Mostly, I just slept late.

"Yeah, my mom says I'm going to have to give something up if I want to be really good at anything, but I want to have options. If the acting doesn't work out, I'll still have my skateboarding and my guitar. I'm not ready to commit, you know? Don't want to limit my opportunities just yet." He turned to watch Kelsey nail the jump. "Wow. She's good."

It was true. Kelsey made skateboarding look incredibly easy.

"You skate?"

"Nah." Watching Kelsey, with her blonde hair flying behind her, and a huge smile on her face made me wish I did. She looked over at me, her two arms stretched gracefully out to her sides, her knees bent, and shouted, "Want to try?"

"I don't think so." But I was willing to be convinced, and Kelsey picked up on my cue.

"Oh come on, it's fun."

Kevin looked at Kelsey. "Let's give her a lesson."

Before I knew it, I was standing on Kevin's board, looking down at my shiny blue toenails in my leather sandals, with Kelsey holding one arm and Dave holding the other. Kevin stood behind me with one hand on each side of my waist.

So there were two firsts at once. I was standing on a skateboard for the first time in my life with a guy's hands on my waist for pretty much the first time in my life. That awful, sweaty slow dance with Arnold Beason in Zann's basement at our eighth grade end-of-the-year party didn't count. Back then, I shuddered in disgust. Now, I was shuddering out of so many different feelings I could hardly sort them out. First, there was the fear of falling, which was connected to the fear of looking like a klutz. Then there was the fear that Kevin would think I was fat. Then there was the utter, indescribable pleasure that ran through my whole body when I felt the weight and warmth of his hands on me. Like being hot and cold at the same time, blushing and shivering all at once.

Thank goodness for Kelsey, for surely I would have fainted or thrown up or something if she hadn't been there, literally propping me up on one side and cheering me on. "Okay, okay. Now look up. Look where you're going!"

So I did, and then Kevin said, right into my ear, "On the count of three, we're going to start moving. One, two, three."

I lurched into Kelsey's side, then over to Dave's. Kevin pressed harder on my waist, which made my knees buckle.

"That's it," said Kelsey, like she was talking to a little kid, "bend your knees. It'll help you get control."

Kevin gave me a little squeeze and let go, running out in front to coach me while the other two held my arms. "Looking good, looking good."

The board was picking up speed, and Dave and Kelsey had to run a little. I yelled out, half in fear for my knees and elbows, not to mention my head, half in the sheer delight of movement. For a second, a brief, brief second, I gave myself over to the moment and stopped thinking so much.

Then I fell. And Kelsey and Dave fell on top of me. And Kevin piled on just for fun. And we all lay there for a few seconds, panting and laughing and breathing each other in.

Then a voice out of nowhere said, "Can I have a turn?" We were laughing so hard we could hardly hear Beka, who had slithered into the school yard without our noticing her.

"Umm, sure," said Kevin, who, as the owner of the board took it upon himself to answer. He disentangled himself and stood up to face Beka. "And you are?"

"Beka. I'm part of the Farnsworth Freak Show,"

she said, using her chin to gesture toward me and Kelsey.

"Hi Beka," said Kelsey. "This is Kevin and Dave."

There were "heys" all around, and the three of us disentangled ourselves. The fabric over one of my knees had torn all the way through, and I'd gotten scraped.

Kevin held his board out to Beka. "Will you be needing a lesson?"

"No thanks," she said as she pushed off with one foot, bent her knees and sailed off down the ramp. She took the jump, too, landing as smoothly as Kelsey had just a few minutes before.

Then Paul and Chris came through the gate and there were more heys and more intros and Beka was demonstrating moves she'd learned in the New York skating scene. Then Kelsey would do what Beka did, always adding a little stylish something like an extra little jump or swerve, which made me kind of proud. No one said anything, but after a few minutes it was obvious that there was a contest going on between the sunny California girl and the dark New York punk.

I sat down on a swing and watched, rooting for Kelsey and watching Kevin watching them. I wondered whether he found Beka interesting. I figured he must, because even though I couldn't stand her, I could see that she was at least interesting. She was wearing her Brady Bunch T-shirt over a sleeveless black leotard, and she also had her dancer's black leggings on under baggy jeans that had been cut off below her knees. She'd put her hair in pigtails and had a plastic Kewpie doll head hanging from one of them.

Between the bubbly Kelsey and gloomy Beka I felt like the least interesting girl on the planet. I turned myself around on the swing so they were all behind me and started swinging. I could still feel the press of Kevin's hands on my waist. I figured that was going to be it for the summer romance, and probably for the rest of my life, so I just closed my eyes and remembered the feeling for a while, until I heard footsteps behind me.

"You're not getting off that easy. Come on, it's time for your next lesson." It was Kevin, holding his board in one hand and holding out his other hand.

I looked back toward the ramp to see that Beka was riding Paul's board now, and that Paul was working on an even more elaborate ramp and jump system that involved milk crates and a picnic table they had up-ended on the concrete steps.

"I can't. I'm injured," I said, pointing to the knee.

"Hah. That's nothing, come on," reaching that empty hand out again.

What could I do but give him mine?

He gripped it firmly and pulled me from the swing. I loosened my grip, but he held on, keeping my hand in his for the whole time it took us to walk back over to the ramp area. Even once we got there it took him a while before letting go.

"It's all in the footing," he said as he placed his board on the ground. "Come on, come on, step up. That's it. Form is very important. Ooh. Nice toes. Here." He actually lifted my left foot and placed it at the front of the board, with the heel facing in slightly, then moved the right foot back, angled the other way.

For the next half hour or so, Kevin and I worked on getting me to think of the board as "an extension of myself." This involved my walking up the ramp over and over again and riding down, with Kevin holding my hand and getting me to bend my knees, shift my hips, and use my shoulders. I never had to use any of the facts I'd memorized from the Plimoth Plantation brochure, and I didn't have to try to think up ways to get him to talk about himself.

In fact, we didn't really talk *about* anything. Mostly we laughed as I kept wobbling my way down the ramp. There was a stretch down at the bottom where I'd pick up speed and where I couldn't help but squeal and he'd talk me through it: "You can do it, Tracy Forrester. Just keep your eyes up and those knees bent. Remember, you and the board are one."

"The board and I are one, the board and I are one, the board and I . . . yikes. I'm gonna fall, I'm gonna fall."

"Okay. Repeat after me, 'I think I can, I think I

can, I think I can.' Didn't they read that to you?"

The Little Engine That Could had, in fact, been my favorite story when I was really little. Most of my books had been hand-me-downs from Chris. But one year, Dad brought home a brand-new copy of *The Little Engine*, along with a read-along cassette just for me, after one of his business trips. I played it over and over until the tape finally broke.

I closed my eyes and chanted, "I think I can, I think I can," along with Kevin. And it did help me catch my balance on the skateboard. And saying it helped me think that maybe I could manage to hold Kevin's interest.

But then I'd catch a glimpse of Kelsey flying off the jump or Beka swerving down the ramp and I'd wonder why in the world Kevin would find me interesting when there were girls like that in the world.

* * *

"So what are you guys doing tomorrow? Dave and I have the day off."

"Um. Umm. Ummm. We're supposed to go to Martha's Vineyard. Another one of Sharon's 'Excursions,'" I said, rolling my eyes.

"Yeah, I know, Sharon the New-Age-Hippie-Mom. She's cool, though. She always lets us hang at her place. Not like some moms, who think we're going to contaminate their houses or something. Plus the food over there. A couple summers ago Sharon gave us all cooking lessons."

Okay. Why was this guy even talking to me? If they put him in one of those magazine articles with a picture and list of all his interests, he'd have thousands of e-mails from girls around the country. I mean, he could act, sing, play guitar, ride a skateboard, *and* cook? This was too much. I considered walking away right there, giving up before my hopes got raised any further. But then he said, "Maybe we can come with you guys." Kevin turned toward Paul and yelled, "Hey, dude, you think your mom'd let us come to the Vineyard with you tomorrow?"

"Yeah man, sure. Mom was just asking about you. We leave at nine."

Kevin cringed. "Nine?" he repeated, looking at me.

Okay, forget it. Of course he'd rather sleep in on his day off than go on some stupid sight-seeing excursion to a place he could go to any time.

"Come for breakfast. We're doing crêpes," Paul yelled over.

"With blueberries?"

"Yup."

"I'll be there," said Kevin. He was answering Paul but looking at me.

Not knowing what else to say, I called out to Kelsey to remind her we'd promised to be home by 8:30. She ran over. She was a little sweaty from all the exertion, but it only made her look even sexier.

"Teach her everything you know?" she asked Kevin.

"Well, we got through the basics. She's got potential," he said smiling at me. "So, we'll see you guys tomorrow."

"Yeah. Tomorrow." And I turned to walk back to Farnsworth House a new woman. A woman with a kinda sorta date for the next day.

Chapter 10

The dads were sitting in the living room with Sharon and Loraine when we got back, pretending to be interested in Emmy, Sammi, and Sean's marathon re-enactment of *The Wizard of Oz*. A cast of three had to work pretty hard to get through the story, passing costumes and props back and forth, whispering lines and stage directions to each other.

"Okay, we're going to have to continue this tomorrow," said my dad as soon as we slammed the screen door behind us.

"No, Daddy, please let us finish," Emmy begged in her sweetest voice.

"Yes, Hank," added Loraine. "*Please, please* let them finish."

"Tell you what, do the ending for us, and you can stay up past your bedtime, just this once." My dad was good at getting Emmy to do things his way and making her think it was her idea.

"You guys turn your backs so we can get in place." The actors huddled and quarreled over whose turn it was to be Dorothy, and finally Emmy lay down on the floor and started talking in her sleep— "I wish I was home, I wish I was home"—and then did a pretty good imitation of Judy Garland's wide-eyed reunion with Auntie Em and Uncle Henry. Everyone clapped when they finished.

Larry yelled, "Bravo!" and whistled a few times and the littles were sent to bed.

Larry and my dad made a big game out of our news that Dave and Kevin wanted to come along to Martha's Vineyard.

"You mean you two would pass up quality time with your dads, your brothers, your marvelous hostess here for a couple of actors?" asked Larry.

"Um, yeah?" Kelsey said.

"Seriously Kels, I don't know these guys," said Larry.

"I do Larry," Sharon offered, all parent-to-parent. "They're Paul's friends. Fine boys. Hard-working, motivated. Like you," she added with a nod and a half wink. "Those jobs at Plymouth are hard to get."

"Hey—time with my kids is hard to get these days, too, right Kelsey?"

"Yeah, Dad. But just because you got divorced and are getting married again doesn't mean I should have to give up having a social life!"

This was the most annoyed I'd heard Kelsey sound in the whole time I'd known her, which I realize wasn't that long at this point. Still, I was surprised, because I really thought she was well adjusted to her parents' divorce. I thought she had arrived at what Mike-the-therapist called "acceptance."

As we were getting ready for bed, I asked her about it. "Oh, yeah, I'm okay with it. I mean, I was sad and everything. But I'm okay with it. My dad feels guilty though, and so every once in a while, when I need to, I use it to get my way. I mean, it's true, right? If they weren't divorced, we wouldn't be at this hippie hotel place. We'd all be living together and I could be seeing my dad and having a social life at the same time."

Beka walked into the room at that point, and so we stopped talking. I didn't think it was possible, but she seemed even meaner than before. She didn't even say any actual words; she just grunted at us while she dug around in her ratty backpack. She took out a prescription vial, twisted it open, and spilled a couple of pills into the palm of her hand. Then she grabbed her toothbrush and toothpaste from the nightstand next to her bed. Beka used a Big Bird toothbrush. One of those really little ones they make for babies. From the looks of it, she might have even had it since she was a baby. The bristles went all over the place. I wasn't sure if this was another example of her "ironic" style, or if it was some kind of security thing.

I didn't dare ask.

When Beka left for the bathroom, Kelsey and I had about two minutes to discuss the evening's events and the next day.

"So, you and Kevin looked like you were having a good time."

"Yeah. I think we were. I mean, I don't think I bored him to death or anything. It was fun learning to skate a little bit. I can kind of see why some guys do it all the time. When you're moving like that, you can kind of forget everything else."

"Yeah. C.J. used to say it was very Zen. 'In the moment' and all that."

Beka came back, plugged herself into her Walkman, and buried herself in her sleeping bag. I wanted to talk a little more about Kevin, but I didn't trust that she wouldn't listen if we were talking. I mean, how would we know if she just turned the volume down and listened to us instead of her music? I'd done that myself a couple of times when I wanted to hear my mom talking on the phone to her mother.

I was pretty sure that what had gone on between me and Kevin was a little more than your usual "just friends" kind of thing. I mean, he seemed to be really attentive and interested in who I was. He even seemed to want to touch me. He didn't seem to mind that of the three girls there, I was the biggest. The last time I'd gone shopping for clothes I'd had to buy size eleven pants. Kelsey was probably a five. And Beka might have even been lower, in the threes or ones, sizes my mom said didn't even exist when she was a teenager.

But as soon as I started to think positively about the situation, I'd remember the downside. He and I lived miles and hours away from each other. I was only going to be here for another week. I'd read articles about summer flings and heard about them from friends. They were always intense. And you went back to school intending to keep up through the phone and e-mail and weekend visits, but someone always lost interest eventually. Then I'd think oh, maybe I should just stay home tomorrow, save everyone the trouble. But I knew I didn't mean it.

* * *

I went back and forth like that for what seemed like hours. Listening to Beka, Kelsey, Sammi, and Emmy snore, I lay on one side imagining these intense, passionate talks Kevin and I would have on the boat to Martha's Vineyard followed by a romantic hand-holding walk on the beach and a stolen kiss on the boat ride back. Then I'd roll over, flip my pillow to the cool side, and picture Kevin so bored by me that he'd jump overboard to escape.

Chapter 11

The last red numbers I remember seeing on the clock by my bed were 2:13, so I was pretty shocked when I opened my eyes to see 8:47 and heard someone calling me.

"Tracy, Tracy, wake up! Everyone's ready to go." This time it was Kelsey pulling on my feet. "You missed a great breakfast. Dave and Kevin cooked with Paul. Blueberry craps."

"I think it's crêpes," I said, using the French pronunciation. I noticed a sweet, buttery breakfast smell in the air and wondered how I had ever managed to sleep through that. "Thanks for waking me up."

"I tried. You were out cold, girl."

I had been hoping to be the first up and have a nice long, hot shower to wake me up. Now I'd have to make it fast, because everyone was waiting. Maybe it was a good thing that all the hot water would be gone. Wake me up.

I didn't have much to choose from clothes-wise. Shorts were out—Kevin might not have minded that I wasn't skinny, but that didn't mean I was ready to expose my legs—as was the long flowery skirt my mom had made me pack for going out to dinner—too frilly. It looked cloudy outside and felt kind of cool, so I decided on my overalls and my "Solo" Brett Smith T-shirt.

I ran down the secret stairs, grabbed a banana from the bowl on the table, and rushed out to the driveway where everyone was standing around. It was warmer than I'd thought, and I considered going back to change when I saw Kevin, Dave, and Paul gathered in a kind of huddle, laughing about something. I dragged my feet on the gravel in the driveway to get Kevin's attention. He looked over at me, and for a second I was afraid he was going to just go right back to talking to the guys. But he didn't. He smiled, waved, and walked over.

"Late night?"

"I don't know what happened. Sorry I missed your crêpes."

"Yeah, well, I guess some people care more about sleeping than eating the best breakfast you could ever have."

Okay. I could do this.

"Really, I don't know what happened. Believe me,

you think I'd rather eat one of these than your crêpes?"

"Snooze you lose, as they say."

Okay. What do I say now?

"Yes. I'm sure it was my loss, entirely. It won't happen again."

"Again? Who says you're going to get another chance to try our wonderful cuisine?"

"Oh. I just . . ." He was kidding, right? We were flirting, or something, right? I wasn't sure anymore. But he wouldn't be standing there looking at me and saying these things if he was really mad or really not interested anymore, right?

"Well, maybe we'll give you another chance. We'll see."

Whew.

*   *   *

Sharon took the teens in the VW, and the littles went with the other parents.

As soon as Sharon started up the van, Chris and Beka plugged themselves in to the Walkman. She wore her Brady Bunch shirt—again. And Chris had on a shirt I'd never seen. It said "Navy Seals" and had an insignia on it, but it had been ripped in several places, and someone had crossed out the S and written in a D with some kind of glittery silver paint so it said "Navy Deals."

Kevin was the first to talk. "Hey, cool shirt," he said

nodding to Chris in the back seat. "What does it mean?'" Chris looked down at the shirt while Beka jumped in, snarling. "It means the navy deals in death." Then she turned up the volume on the Walkman, crossed her arms in front of her chest, and sat back to listen to "Uncle Damn."

"Oh, okay. Cool." Kevin turned back to me with a raised eyebrow. He lowered his voice to ask, "Is she like that all the time?"

"Well . . ." I was a little stumped by the question. Overnight, it seemed that Beka had become even angrier. Her black eyeliner was thicker than usual, and she wore these heavy lace-up boots. Glancing back casually, hoping she wouldn't see me looking at her, I saw that she'd added horns to Peter Brady's head.

As Beka had gotten punkier, Kelsey had gone even more California golden-girl. Today's outfit consisted of stretchy orange capris with a "Girls Rule" T-shirt. She'd painted her toenails a shimmery green and wore those clunky flip-flops with a thin beaded ankle bracelet and a silver toe ring. Toes and ankles were parts of my body I'd never even considered accessorizing.

"Angry girl," Kevin whispered.

"What?" I was totally confused, until I realized that while I was studying Kelsey, Kevin was still on Beka.

"Oh, yeah. I'll say."

I would have thought that now that Kelsey had shifted her attention away from Paul, Beka'd back off a little bit. But Dave's being here as Kelsey's sort-of date only seemed to make Beka even angrier. Because despite Kelsey's apparent preference for Dave, Paul's attention hadn't turned back to Beka.

In fact, Paul didn't seem the least bit bothered by Dave's status as Kelsey's "date." The three of them were deep into a conversation about the skateboarder's life.

It started with Kelsey telling them about her ex, C.J., and the skate park where he trained.

"You guys have a skate park? Man. I gotta get out to Cali," said Paul.

"Yeah, it's pretty cool. Now we don't have to worry about getting busted at the school yard. Berkeley cops are pretty cool, though. At least the ones on bikes. Mostly they just asked us to leave, even if they had just asked us the same thing the day before. You can stay at our house if you want to check it out. I'll introduce you to C.J. Oh, and no one in California says 'Cali.' Or 'Frisco.' If we're going to San Francisco, we just say 'The City.'"

Beka made a sputtering sound of disapproval. So she had been listening. "Sorry Kelsey, but New York is 'The City.'"

Kelsey didn't bite. "Oh. I guess it depends on where you are when you say it."

"Yeah, Beka, out here people mean Boston when they say 'The City,'" said Paul, pretty much putting an end to her attempt to enter the conversation.

"Is there room for me at your house?" Dave asked Kelsey.

"Sure. We've got people staying at our house all the time. My mom and grandparents are really cool about that as long as you pick up after yourself."

I looked back to see Beka still staring out the window, her face as angry as ever.

I was completely baffled by it all. It had looked to me like both Dave and Paul were interested in Kelsey, but they were also really good friends. They wanted Kelsey to like them, but they also liked each other.

The only thing that was clear to me sitting there watching though, was that Kelsey was having a good time. And Paul and Dave were having a good time. No one seemed to be thinking about things quite as much as I was. Well, except maybe Beka.

It was impossible for me to not think. I was sitting there trying to remember the list of ten things you were supposed to do on a first date to make sure you had a second, which I'd read in *Seventeen* at the dentist's office earlier in the summer. They had interviewed ten different guys, who each offered his own unique tip. Stuff like, "'Show your inner beauty,' says Jason of San Jose, California. 'Yeah, man, chemistry is important, don't get me wrong. But I gotta see some soul, too.'" Or "'Don't be afraid to show your brainpower,'" from Ryan in Wisconsin. "'My grandma told me that when she was young, her mother told her to pretend to be dumber than she was, so she wouldn't scare off the guys. Well, my grandma was too smart for that, and it's a good thing, too, 'cause it was her brains that interested my grandpa. And if those two had never gotten together, then I wouldn't be here today talking to you. I like smart girls.'" Over his quote they had a model dressed in a white lab coat and the funkiest, most up-to-the-minute glasses.

So I was sitting there, wondering how to let Kevin know that I had soul and brainpower when some rather loud rustling started up in the back seat.

I caught a glimpse of Beka's black bra as she pulled a T-shirt over her head and rolled it down over her chest and stomach. "There. Now I'm ready for Martha's Vineyard," she announced proudly and loudly, jutting back her shoulders.

The conversation stopped while everyone turned to look.

After about fifteen seconds of utter silence, Paul spoke. "Ah, Beka, that's really not cool."

"Definitely. Not. Cool," said Kevin, shaking his head, raising his eyebrows and looking her in the eye, kind of like he was talking to a little sister.

"What? The Dead Kennedys were like one of the biggest punk bands of the eighties. Do you know how hard it is to find these shirts? This is an original. You can't buy an authentic one anywhere in New York. The guy in the thrift store gave it to me for thirty bucks. I talked him down from fifty."

Paul, Dave, and Kevin exchanged a look. Then it was Dave's turn to take on the big-brother role. "Beka, Jake Shipper's brother owns a T-shirt factory. They track down rare T-shirts, scan the design in on their computer, and create a new screen. They wash them in this really lethal acid stuff to make them look old, and then they sell 'em to tourist kids like you for oh, about twenty times what it cost them to make. He'll be displaying another 'vintage original' in a couple weeks, when he's sure you've left town."

"But besides being a fake, Beka," continued Paul, "it's just not cool. I mean, do the math. It hasn't even been two years." He was talking about J.F.K. Jr.'s plane crash, of course, which, if you were over the age of, say, eight, and living in the United States, you couldn't help but know about. I couldn't believe that anyone, even Beka, could be so heartless.

Beka opened her mouth to argue, but Paul cut her off.

"You're not getting out of the Farnsworth House van wearing that. It's just not cool."

"Not cool," echoed Kevin.

"Not cool," added Dave.

Sharon was silent. Once in a while she'd glance back at Beka through her rearview.

Before this moment, I wouldn't have been able to imagine Paul mad. He just always seemed to take things lightly. Even when he was complaining about the cops harassing him and his skating buddies, there was always a sense that he liked the cops and knew that they were just doing their job. But now he was looking at her with true disgust.

"Chill out, Paul. Jeez, What are you, my mother? I thought you had a sense of humor. I thought you understood irony."

"Sure, I have a sense of humor, when things are funny. And irony—I'm sure you know—is supposed to make a point. When Jello Biafra named his band, John Kennedy had been dead for what? fifteen years? Bobby for ten. They were pushing it, trying to rile people up by attacking the sacred Kennedys. But really, a lot's happened since then. I mean, have some respect. People on Martha's Vineyard will not appreciate your irony, believe me. They'll just think you're stupid."

The shoulders Beka'd been holding out proudly just a moment before fell into a definite slump. She looked at Chris, who was looking out the window, then at Paul, who was staring right at her, and Dave and Kevin who were shaking their heads in that big-brother-to-little-sister way.

I thought I saw Beka's bottom lip start to tremble. But before I could be sure, she ducked behind the seat again.

We could hear her mumbling as we watched an elbow come up and then down again. The offending shirt was hurled into the luggage area of the van. As she sat back up, Beka muttered something about Cape Cod being "like fucking Wisconsin." She had the old

Brady shirt on again. She plugged herself into her Walkman, folded her arms over her chest, and stared out the window.

A few minutes later, Sharon announced our arrival at Falmouth Harbor.

Chapter 12

"Come on kids," said Kevin, "we'll show you where the captain steers the boat." Emmy, Sammi, and Josh hopped out of the back seat, but Sean had to be coaxed.

"Come on, you, too. I'll show you how to feed the seagulls."

When Kevin said that, Sean's eyes lit up, and he cracked a smile for the first time all week. "Really? Do you have any Alka-Seltzer? I hear they explode if you feed 'em Alka-Seltzer."

"Oh ho, nice. No, we're not going to make seagull bombs. Jeez. How old are you, anyway?"

"Six." Sean was trying to look sullen again, but I saw him crane his neck to sneak a look at Kevin as we walked toward the steps at the end of the dock.

When we got to the front of the line, Paul's friend

Andy, another skinny, sun-blond guy with a deep tan, treated him like teen royalty. "Dude! I haven't seen you since last year. 'Sup? You still ska-eightin'?" He was shaking Paul's hand but looking at Kelsey.

"Oh yeah. You should come down some time. We've got some excellent jumps in the old school yard."

"Cool. Cool," he said absently as he returned his eyes toward Kelsey. "Aren't you going to introduce me to your friends?"

"Oh, yeah, sorry. Kelsey, Chris, Beka, Tracy, Emmy, Sammi, and Sean—meet first mate Andy Taylor. They're here for 'Together Time.'"

"Your mom's still doing that divorced parent thing?"

"Oh yeah. It's the highlight of her summer."

"I might have to come down, you know my parents've been fighting a lot lately."

"Yeah?"

"Yeah. Maybe I need to come around and hang out with all the rest of you children of divorce." Again, he started out talking to Paul, but ended up looking at Kelsey, who didn't seem to notice.

As the conversation took off on a new track, the woman behind us, who was holding one little kid in her arms and another by the hand said, "Excuse me, but do you think you guys could catch up after we're all on board? If my kid doesn't get to a bathroom some time in the next sixty seconds . . ."

Andy looked truly apologetic as he said, "Sure, sure, sorry, ma'am. We just hadn't seen each other in a while. Go on up. Later, dude."

"Later. Don't forget to come down on your day off. We're there every night after dinner."

Andy snuck one more look at Kelsey as he said, "Cool, yeah, I'll come by."

*   *   *

The boat was huge, and pretty old, with a parking area for cars, then two levels for passengers. The first floor had an enclosed area with a snack bar and tables, or you could sit outside on either the front or back of the boat. Paul led us to the top deck, which was totally open.

"We'll see the most from up there."

Beka and Chris said they'd rather stay downstairs.

Dave and Kelsey took the little kids over to see where the captain steered the boat.

Paul found yet another crew member he knew and went off to talk to him.

Which left me and Kevin alone together for the first time all morning.

"Pretty tense ride, huh?" he said.

"Yeah. Beka's very dramatic. Makes scenes everywhere we go."

"I know the type. Pissed at the world. My sister has a friend like that, Arianna. Goes into these snit fits all the time. Very high maintenance."

That's what I didn't get about girls like Beka and this Arianna person Kevin was talking about. High maintenance types never had any trouble getting boyfriends. The angriest girl at my school, Helen Green, had a new one every couple of months. It seemed like the more grief she gave each one, the faster they'd line up to take over when she dumped them. And she always dumped them. There was even an unofficial club—guys who called themselves "X Greens." As soon as one of them got dumped, the others would welcome him by making a big green X on his locker. Then they'd all get drunk together and trade stories.

I could see why someone like Kelsey would have guys lining up for her, but the Bekas, Helens, and Ariannas of this world I just did not get.

Where was Kelsey anyway? I needed her to help me get things rolling with Kevin. I didn't know what to say now that we were standing here alone. I didn't really want to talk about Beka anymore, but I didn't know what else to talk about. Last night at the playground things just flowed, and even this morning on the driveway things seemed promising. But now I was completely paralyzed.

I looked across the deck to see Kelsey standing and laughing with the little kids and Paul, Dave, and the captain of the ferry.

"So, this your first trip to the Vineyard?" asked Kevin.

"Apparently I was here once as a baby. We used to visit my grandparents at their house in Orleans, and my mother says we went to the Vineyard when I was three. I don't remember. So it may as well be."

Kevin nodded, but he was looking across the deck at the kids feeding the gulls. Could I be any more boring? Kelsey didn't have this trouble keeping a conversation going. And as angry as she was, even Beka knew how to keep a guy's attention. She was interesting.

"How about you?" I asked, remembering the rule about getting them to talk about themselves.

"What?" He had to think for a second. "Oh. We come out every fall with our bio teacher to study the tide pools. But no one who lives on the Cape goes to the Vineyard during the summer, when all the um, tourists are around."

"You mean, like people from Farnsworth House?"

"Well, no, you guys don't count. You're Paul's friends. You're cool."

"Wouldn't want to embarrass you or anything."

"Oh. No, hey man, I didn't mean that."

Okay. So I'd managed to sustain a somewhat flirtatious exchange for what? like two seconds. Then I just ran out of ideas. I panicked. I needed a lifeline.

"Hey, let's go see what those guys are doing," I said, and started across the deck. Kevin just stood there for a minute, and then he followed me.

When Kevin had first used the word "captain," I'd

pictured an old guy with a beard in a white uniform. Well, this guy looked to be in his twenties. He wore the same bright yellow windbreaker with the ferry authority logo on the front that all the crew wore. He was lifting up the little kids one by one to stand in front of the big steering wheel. Sean reached out to touch something on the electronic dashboard and the captain guy said, "Whoa. Whoa. Do not touch anything little man."

"Is this your radar?" asked Sean, his fingers hovering just above the buttons below the monitor.

"Yes, it's the radar," he answered, firmly pushing Sean's hand away from the instrument panel. "Hey Paul, can you take your little campers out now? I gotta get this boat moving."

"Sure man, come on campers. You heard the captain. Now say, 'Aye, aye, Captain,'" Paul held his hand up to his forehead in a pretend salute, "and 'Thank you,' and we'll go feed the seagulls."

Emmy, Sammi, and Sean obeyed Paul's instructions and craned their necks up at the captain, and filed out of the tiny space. Josh offered his hand for shaking and, I thought, to make sure the captain knew he wasn't one of the little kids.

Just then the engine roared up and the boat started pulling out of its berth. Very slowly. It was only by staring at the docked ferry next to us that I could be sure we were moving.

I got kind of hypnotized doing that. I was smelling

the salt air and liking it again, not feeling all sad about our lost summers at our grandparents. I could hear the crying of the seagulls and the horn blast of the ferry as it pulled out, and for a minute, I felt hopeful. I was traveling with a group that included three cute guys, one of whom seemed to kind of maybe like me. And then there was Kelsey. I was sure that if we lived in the same town we'd be best friends—or maybe she and Zann and I could be a threesome of best friends. We'd hang out in Kelsey's room spying on her grandmother's clients as they left her office weeping. And we'd talk over our crushes and share our sadness about our parents.

"Hello?"

It took me a few seconds to pull out of that trance and turn Kevin's way.

"Earth to Tracy. Wow. Where were you?"

"Oh. I don't know. I just kind of spaced."

"I'll say, you looked like you were on another planet. Wanna go feed the gulls with them?" He gestured up to the front of the boat where Paul was holding out a piece of bread while about twenty white-and-gray gulls floated and flapped and dived at him.

I said, "No."

But I didn't mean, "No I don't want to be with you." I meant, "I would rather stand here with you, just the two of us, talking or trying to talk or whatever it is we're doing." So then I tried to clarify by saying, "I'd kind of like to sit here spacing out some more." But I left out "with you," thinking it wasn't necessary, and also because I was afraid to say something so blatant.

He shrugged. "Okay. Well, I'll be over there with those guys." And he walked away.

I sat down, closed my eyes, and put my face to the sun. But the happy-hopeful feeling was long gone. I found myself watching Kevin with one eye and trying to find inner peace with the other closed tight. He sidled up alongside Paul, grabbed some bread out of the brown bag Paul and Sharon had packed, and tossed a handful of bread up into the air, sending the birds flying every which way. Soon he was chattering away with—who else?—Kelsey, supporting her arm as she held a piece of bread up for the voracious flock of seagulls.

Then I saw him throw a piece of bread straight down to the deck below. As soon as he'd done it, he pulled his head back behind the railing, as if he was hiding from someone. He waited a few seconds, then took another piece of bread and did the same thing, laughing all the while.

"Watch out dude," said Paul. "You're playing with fire there."

I'm not sure why I looked, because I already knew who I would see when I peeked over the railing to find Kevin's target. Sure enough, there she was, picking crumbs out of her dark hair, scowling and swearing and arousing the interest of all around her.

Chapter 13

I knew we were there when I spotted the Gingerbread Houses Sharon had told us about.

Oak Bluffs' other big claim to fame was this hundred-year-old carousel called the Flying Horses. The little kids had been bribed out of whining in the car with promises of a ride as soon as we got off the boat. After that, and our box lunches, we were going to be given options for activities—all of which, the parents had agreed, would be chaperoned. Thanks to Chris and Beka's little encounter with the Provincetown Police, my first kind-of date would be complete with adult supervision.

I felt like I'd pretty much blown it already, like Kevin had already discovered just how boring I was. But when I heard the organ music and saw all those tiny lightbulbs on the carousel, I got all hopeful again.

This merry-go-round was like no other I'd seen before. Each horse was painted a little differently from the others, and they had such expressive faces. Some were made to look like they were galloping, others trotting. All were beautiful.

"Get one for me, too!" I shouted to my dad, who had volunteered to get on the ticket line.

"Me too!" shouted Kelsey.

"Get one for everybody, Hank," said Sharon. She gazed at the circling horses. "We used to spend hours here when Paul was little." She turned to Kevin. "Remember when your mom and I took you guys here and you threw up all over everything?"

"Gee, thanks for that little trip down memory lane. Would you like to tell everyone about changing my diapers while you're at it?" Then, turning to me, he said, "Why do they always do that? I mean, my mom's not even here and you're getting the stupid-things-I-did-when-I-was-little stories."

So maybe I hadn't blown it.

The place was mobbed, every horse taken for each of the three rides we waited through before our turn. I studied the crowd. There were the usual families with a mom and a dad and one or two children. Here and there I saw just a mom with her kids or just a dad, and I had to wonder whether the dad was over at the snack bar or at work or maybe living in some completely different place from his kids, or whether the missing mom was taking a nap back at the hotel or if she was wandering around an empty house while her kids were on vacation with her ex-husband.

I thought for sure Beka and Chris would pass on riding the carousel, too cool to be seen doing such a thing in the company of their families. But they didn't. Beka, in fact, got on a yellow horse right next to the black one I chose for myself. Kevin hopped on the brown one on the other side of me. Kelsey and Dave sat in the stationary bench together. The only person who didn't want to ride was Loraine, who said she was still recovering from the ferry.

"Oh, come on, Mom, don't be chicken." Beka's tone was playful and inviting. It was the kindest thing I'd heard her say to her mother in the whole time I'd known them. "Here, sit behind me on this guy," she said, patting the nose of a white-and-gray horse. "He's so sweet."

Looking surprised by her usually surly daughter's invitation, Loraine hoisted herself into the saddle. "I better not get sick. If I do, I'm blaming you."

"You'll be fine, Mom. If you feel queasy, just stare at the horse's ears. That's what you taught me to do when I was little, remember?"

"Yeah, I do honey." Loraine's voice softened as she looked at her daughter before her. "It wasn't that long ago."

The bell rang and the organ started in on "Bicycle Built for Two," a tune I knew from my early piano lessons. It was one of Mrs. Finch's favorites. She said it was good for practicing rhythm. She used to sing along while I practiced, swaying back and forth on the bench with me. Apparently Dave and Kevin had had a goofy music teacher, too, because they knew all the words, and sang out in their booming actor-guy voices.

Daisy, Daisy, give me your answer, do.
I'm half crazy, all for the love of you. . . .

Everyone sitting near us and even some of the people waiting in line laughed and clapped when they were done. But when they started in on the next song, "That Daring Young Man on the Flying Trapeze," someone complained.

"Hey come on guys, can we just hear the organ this time? It's part of the experience, you know?" Just behind me, Beka, and Kevin was the lady from the ferry line. Her two kids were sitting on the horses next to Loraine, and she was standing between them, her feet spread out for balance, her hands resting on top of two horses' manes.

Even though she'd been lectured by these guys just an hour before, Beka—always ready for a fight—rushed to their defense. "Oh, come on lady, lighten up. Your kids are loving it."

"Well, I'm not. I would just like to hear the organ music and be able to talk to my kids. That's what we came here for, right kids? You wanted to hear the music Mommy used to hear when she was little."

Her children, a boy and girl who looked like they were maybe three and five, stared back at her without speaking. I wondered where the dad was.

"Who the fuck cares about you? Huh? Do you think the world revolves around you and your little brats?"

"Beka!" Loraine shouted from behind. Then she turned toward the woman, whose eyes had widened at Beka's sudden eruption. "I'm so sorry."

"*I'm* not sorry. Mom, don't apologize for me." Turning toward the woman, Beka continued, "This woman is mean. And stupid."

The little boy yelled back at Beka, "You're not supposed to say stupid!" then turned to his mother, "Mommy she said stupid! She should have a time-out."

Loraine tried to lower her voice as she said, mother-to-mother "She's having a rough time. I am really so sorry." But the carousel music made it impossible to speak quietly, and of course, Beka heard it.

Boy was that the wrong thing to say.

"No I am not having a fucking rough time. It was funny! They were having a little fun. Everyone was having a little fun and then this—this," Beka glanced at the boy who had just lectured her and continued, "this *woman* has to go and spoil everything."

The man who operated the machine sat on a tall stool in the center. He'd been watching us, laughing when Dave and Kevin were singing. Now, he kept his eye on Beka until her horse circled out of sight. She was still spewing when we came back around, and he stretched his arm out to pull the switch he'd pulled to get us going. The carousel had barely begun to slow down when Beka stood up on the fake stirrups, swung her leg over her horse, and hopped off. Then, using the other horses to brace herself, she made her way to the edge. The guy on the stool shouted, "Hey! No walking while the carousel is moving!" But it was no use. She leapt, ballerina-like, first one leg and then the other. She landed gracefully on the ground—with just the slightest bounce.

My brain had the weirdest thought, *Wow, Beka is a really good dancer.*

We were still circling, and by the time we came back around to where she had landed, she was gone. Paul, Dave, and Kevin jumped off looking like some out-of-practice teenage superheroes—Dave and Kevin fell into each other, making the little kids laugh. Paul extended each of his arms out and pulled them both to standing. Then Chris jumped off, too, making the dynamic trio into a quartet. By the time we went one more time around and stopped, the four of them were out of sight.

The whole place got really quiet for a minute. The music stopped. And everyone was looking at Loraine, who sat holding her head in her hands.

The woman who started it all was the first to speak. "Come on sweeties, let's go get some lunch." Something about her tone made me start to side with Beka in her hatred. And when the woman turned to another mother with a small child and said, "They ought to make this a kids-only place, or only let the teenagers on after dark or something," I was convinced Beka was right. The woman was mean and stupid.

Loraine sat there, slumped over her horse, obviously upset, and the mother just went right on, rubbing it in. "You're right Hunter, you're not supposed to call people stupid. That girl was rude."

And I couldn't help feeling sorry for Loraine, whose daughter had gone from fun-loving kid to hate-spewing teen in the space of two minutes, who had to endure the icy stares of the two mothers as they lifted their children off the horses and scurried away, as if just sitting next to the mother of the bad girl might contaminate their kids.

Sharon was at Loraine's side immediately. I hadn't even seen her walk over from her horse a few rows back.

"The boys'll find her, honey. Don't worry."

Then I saw that Loraine was crying. Full-on. Blotchy-faced, snot and all. Sharon put her arm around her and Loraine buried her face in Sharon's flowery sundress. She was sobbing so hard that she shook Sharon's body, too.

Patting Loraine's back, Sharon said, "Come on, it'll be okay. She's a live one, Loraine, that's for sure. But she's going to be okay. You know, I was a little like her at her age."

Five days ago, I don't think Loraine would have taken that as a good sign. But things seemed to be loosening up between her and Sharon. She nodded and almost smiled.

Larry walked up next to Sharon, and together the two of them half lifted, half pulled Loraine down off her horse. For a minute it was like Sharon was Loraine's mother, holding her close while directing her toward the exit. The rest of us lined up behind Sharon, Larry, and Loraine and slunked out. People tried not to stare but they did, until the guy unhooked the chain at the front of the line and started the music up again.

As we filed out into the sun, the carousel arcade returned to what it had been when we arrived. Full of noisy families waiting their turn to make the memories. As I watched the moms and dads with their one or two kids, I wondered which ones would stay together and which ones would break up. I wondered how old the kids would be when their dads moved out; which ones would be the scene-makers like Beka and which would be the watchers like me.

✳ Chapter 14 ✳

An hour went by without a sign of Beka.

The boys divided the crowd into quadrants, a search-and-rescue method Chris had learned in the Boy Scouts. It was a good idea, because then we could be reasonably sure that Beka wasn't in the immediate vicinity of the carousel. But I couldn't help wondering what Beka would have said if she knew

a.) That Chris had been a Boy Scout.

b.) That he was using Boy Scouts of America techniques to try to find her.

Shuttle buses left from the docks every fifteen minutes. If she'd hopped on one of those, Beka could have been on the other side of the island by now. Or she could have gotten back on the ferry and headed over to Falmouth. We had no idea.

Two bike-riding cops in shorts, blue T-shirts with

yellow insignias over their hearts, and mirrored cop sunglasses told Loraine they couldn't do anything official unless Beka was missing for twenty-four hours or committed a crime like shoplifting or hitchhiking. Leaping off the historical Oak Bluffs carousel didn't merit an arrest warrant. But they did radio in a report and told Loraine that the other cops around the island would keep a look out for her.

"They usually turn up by the end of the day, ma'am," offered the one with the salt-and-pepper mustache, who looked old enough to have a teenager or two of his own. "They get hungry, you know? And bored. She'll come back. She done this before?"

Loraine shook her head. "Well. Back home. She storms out for an afternoon now and then. And once she spent the night at a friends'." She paused to sniffle, and continued, "But I knew where she was because the friend's mother called me. I let her pretend she had run away, and she let me pretend to punish her when she got back."

"She have any money on her?"

"Oh, I don't know. Maybe ten dollars."

I thought of Beka's saying she bought the Dead Kennedys T-shirt for thirty and wondered if Loraine really knew enough about her daughter to know how much money she had in her pockets.

The officer nodded knowingly. "Oh, she'll be back."

* * *

So the older kids and the adults took turns searching through the crowd, some of us staying behind with the little ones, who were cranky, bored, and scared. They were used to their older siblings fighting with their parents, but they hadn't seen anything quite this dramatic.

"Does Beka know how to swim, Loraine?" asked Emmy, trying to make it sound like a simple question.

It took Loraine a while to realize someone was talking to her. "What? Oh? Yes, Emmy, Beka's an excellent swimmer, don't you worry about that. She can take really good care of herself, too. At this point, I'm more worried about everyone else than I am about her."

She stood up from the bench where she had been sitting next to Sharon and peered off into the crowd, hands on her hips.

"I am not going to let that girl out of my sight for the rest of this vacation."

"Then you'll be punishing yourself," said Sharon, who came up from behind and put a hand on Loraine's shoulder. "Why don't you just wait until we have her back here before you decide what to do, huh? Maybe you two can have a talk. Maybe some good can come of this."

"But I can't just let her get away with it. She's spoiled the day for everyone now."

"Maybe not. Listen, why don't I take the little kids and Tracy and Kelsey over to Vineyard Haven? They've got an interesting little museum, and a great lighthouse. We'll take our lunches, and you can call us on Kelsey's cell phone if anything happens."

So now my "date," if we could still apply the term to this disaster of a social situation, was totally over. Kevin hadn't said much to me since that moment on the ferry when I'd said that stupid stuff about wanting to space out, and now he and Dave were too busy playing teenage *Mission Impossible* to notice me and Kelsey. They'd set up this little command central on the other bench, spreading a map of the island against its back and studying shuttle bus schedules, trying to figure out how far Beka could have gone. Chris gave them a quick lesson in using their shadows to navigate by the sun.

Meanwhile, my dad went over to meet the ferry that was just coming in, to see if Beka might have been planning to cross back to the mainland. Larry found a bicycle shop and rented bikes for him and Josh. They headed out along the main road that crossed the island, figuring if Beka were on foot, they'd overtake her.

Sharon's plan sounded better than hanging out in front of the carousel watching all the men scurry after Beka. The organ sound track had played through a few times now, getting more annoying each time. I'd seen enough cute three- and four-year-olds and seemingly happy couples to last the entire vacation. I couldn't have cared less about the stupid lighthouse and museum, but it would beat sitting around waiting.

I forced myself into helpful mode. "Who wants to go see a lighthouse?"

"We do! We do!" shouted Sammi and Emmy.

"I *don't*," protested Sean, with a stomp of his foot. "I want to stay *here* with my *mom*."

Loraine was staring out into the crowd, as though Beka might just come walking back to her any minute. "Honey, I'm okay. Please go with Sharon and the girls. I bet that by the time you get back, Beka will be here, too."

"But Mom . . ."

"No buts, honey, now go."

Registering his protest with pursed lips and crossed arms, Sean turned away from his mother and toward me. Without thinking, I put my hand out and, before I knew it, he and I were walking hand-in-hand toward the shuttle bus stop. Kelsey held out her hands for Sammi and Emmy.

"I know what a lighthouse is," Sean declared.

"Oh yeah?"

"Yeah," he explained, sounding a little like Loraine in schoolteacher mode. "They're from the old days, when they didn't have radar. They're like gigantic flashlights and they have really loud horns. So that the boats won't crash on the rocks."

"That's a pretty good way of explaining it."

"Yeah. I know a lot of stuff. Do you know if the lighthouse still works?"

"I don't know. We can ask when we get out there."

"Yeah," said Sean. "Maybe they can help us find Beka, if she's still out when it gets dark."

"Yeah, maybe."

* * *

The shuttle bus left us off on Main Street in front of the Old Schoolhouse Museum. There was a tall pole, with a historical plaque dedicated to "the patriotism of three girls of this village: Polly Daggett, Parnel Manter, Maria Allen, who destroyed with powder a liberty pole erected near this spot." Sharon filled me in on the story of how these three teenagers blew up the original pole so that the British Army, which had invaded Martha's Vineyard, couldn't use it for their warship.

As the little kids ran around on the lawn and Kelsey set out down Main Street in search of coffee, I tried to imagine myself, along with Kelsey and the only other teenage girl around, Beka, doing something so daring. In my mind it played out like some cheesy TV show. We were wearing long, tight-fitting dresses and little bonnets. Our faces were smeared with dirt, but were also perfectly made-up.

To make it more dramatic, I imagined that the boys—Dave, Kevin, Paul, and Chris—were kind of our rivals, that we were competing with them to see who could thwart the enemy's plans first. Of course, it being the Revolutionary War and all, no one would expect three teenage girls to pull off such a task. But we would win in the end, and win the boys' undying love and admiration as well.

While I was cooking up the pilot for my Revolutionary War teen series on the W.B., Sharon came up beside me.

"Kind of makes you think, huh?"

"What do you mean?"

"I mean, can you imagine, first of all, having your home burned to the ground by an invading army? An army that spoke the same language as you, from a place that your parents or grandparents had once called home?"

One of the houses on our street had a fire a few years ago. It happened in the middle of the night, and we all went out to watch the firemen, but we didn't really see much. Just a bunch of guys in their yellow coats, a little smoke, and the Jenner family in their pajamas, crying. "No, I really can't," I said.

"Okay. Close your eyes."

"Why?"

"Just do what I say. Close your eyes. Good. Now, smell the air. What do you smell?"

"I don't know, salt? Popcorn?" I could smell food anywhere.

"Okay. Forget all that. Concentrate on the ocean smell. Now, imagine that none of this is here. All around you are a few farms, some big family homes, the schoolhouse where you learned to spell your name and where you and your friends ran around during recess. You've watched your parents work hard to provide you with food and shelter. Your father gets up early in the morning to work the fields while your mother's baking that day's bread."

I was trying. But Sharon's story got me thinking about how mornings used to be at our house. How I'd lie in bed hearing the sounds of my father taking a shower, my mother making the coffee while she listened to the news on our old kitchen radio. How I used to hear them talking, then when I got a little older, sniping at each other over whose turn it was to do what. Then, when it got closer to the time they broke up, not talking at all except to say, "Excuse me," or "Are there any more Corn Flakes?" or "Are you finished with that section?" Always polite but icy with each other at the end.

"Now, imagine a boat full of angry men with guns come in and take all that away from you. They order you out of your house, and then, after taking all the food from the pantry, they burn it to the ground. They shoot the cow you've been milking every morning and cook up the meat for their dinner that night. They take your mother's homemade strawberry preserves and eat them straight from the jar, throwing what they don't want on the floor."

I wasn't quite doing what Sharon was trying to get me to do—feel what those girls must have felt—angry enough to risk their own lives for their country. But I was feeling something. By the time she told me to open my eyes again, I was crying, not for the teenage heroines the memorial celebrated, but for my parents, who had lost whatever it was that made them think they would spend their lives together. Whatever it was that made them think it was a pretty safe bet to have not one or two but three children who they now had to take turns taking care of.

Before I knew it, Sharon had me in her big hippie arms, and I was pressed against the flowered sundress Loraine had been crying into a couple hours ago. Something about the way Sharon did it just let you kind of let go.

I thought back to those mornings I lay half awake, hearing my parents not talk to each other. And I thought back to those times when I was really little, how I'd wake up in the middle of the night and head into their room and find them all tangled up together, how hot my mother's body felt when she carried me back to my room and said, "Mommy and Daddy want to sleep alone tonight, honey. As soon as you wake up and see light out the window, you can come back in and snuggle with us."

I knew it wasn't exactly what Sharon was getting at, but at that moment, I thought that if there had been something I could blow up to keep my parents from falling out of love with each other I would have done it. I would have snuck out of the house late at night and scattered gunpowder around it, and lit the match and run.

Chapter 15

"Hey you guys, I scored," said Kelsey, carrying a cardboard tray full of clear plastic bubble-top cups piled high with whipped cream. "No Starbucks, but I found frozen mochas at this cute little place."

The three of us—Sharon, Kelsey, and I—sat down on the grass across from the liberty pole and drank our sweet treats and nibbled at our tuna sandwiches.

"I hope you got decaf," said Sharon.

"Yours is, ours aren't." Kelsey looked at me with a sneaky smile. "There isn't that much caffeine in these things anyway."

My mother never let me drink anything but hot chocolate or orange juice when we went to coffee places at home. It was terrible, but just after this dramatic daydream of saving my family from the enemy of divorce, I was sitting on a sunny lawn in a beautiful town on Martha's Vineyard, enjoying something I would never be allowed to have if we were on a real family vacation with my mother and father.

Emmy, Sammi, and Sean had found a playground and had retreated into that kids-only world of pretend. I heard Emmy ordering the others around. "Okay. Now, I'm the mommy and you're my kids. You're twins, and I'm going to push you on the swings."

"I don't want to be a kid," Sean protested. "I'll be the daddy."

"No," said Emmy. "There's no daddy. He got a divorce."

Kelsey's cell phone rang. She looked at the caller-ID screen, said, "It's my dad," and pushed the talk button. "Did you find her? Oh. Uh-huh. Uh-huh. When?" Sharon and I stared as she looked at her watch and then back toward the bus stop. "Okay. Yeah. Okay."

"She's back. We're supposed to meet them at the ferry as soon as we can get back there."

"Wait a second," said Sharon. "We're not going to let a little temper tantrum ruin our outing. Let me see that phone, Kelsey." She extended her arm and Kelsey obeyed, looking at me and shrugging her shoulders. "What's your dad's number?"

Kelsey told her, but after trying to press a few of the tiny buttons Sharon handed it back. "You dial."

"Oh, you don't have to dial." Kelsey pushed the talk button twice and then said, "Dad, cell," slowly and clearly, like she was talking to an old person who couldn't hear well. She held it to her ear for a second and then handed it back to Sharon. "It's ringing." Then Kelsey turned to me and said, "This is kind of fun, just the two of us and Sharon."

"And them," I said, gesturing with my chin toward the little kids, who had abandoned *Divorced Family* and were now acting out *The Wizard of Oz* again.

"Yeah, and them. They're okay."

"But what about Dave and Kevin—our so-called dates?"

"Oh, we'll catch up with them later. At the playground after dinner. It'll be good to keep them waiting."

"Okay, if you say so." My instinct would have been to get back to that boat as soon as possible. Of course, when I got there, I would probably still not know how to talk to Kevin any better than I was doing before. Kelsey was clearly not worried about "getting" or "losing" Dave or Paul for that matter.

Sharon was mostly saying uh-huh, uh-huh, and asking short questions like, "Where?" "That far, huh?" and "Really?" She told Larry to take everyone back in the VW. Paul had a spare key. Then she told them to leave a key for the station wagon with the manager of the ferry terminal, who was her friend. Then, in a lowered voice which we could hear perfectly well she said, "You take care of Loraine, Larry, okay?" Then she laughed. "Yeah. We'll see you at dinner time. We'll make tonight pizza night. Tell Paul to call the order in.

Yeah. Invite the boys to stay, okay?" She fiddled with the buttons for a while before giving up and handing the little phone back to Kelsey.

"These things scare me. But I can see how they'd come in handy. I'm still banning them from the house though. You'll have to go out on the driveway if you want to talk on a cell phone or smoke a cigarette at Farnsworth House."

She filled us in on the details. Apparently, the boys ran into a friend of a friend of Paul's, who took them around in his car to look for Beka. They found her out on the road that went to Aquinnah and the Indian reservation where we were going to hike. Beka said she just wanted to be alone for a while, so she figured she'd meet up with everyone out there. As if. As if she thought we'd just go on our merry way after her flying leap off the Flying Horses.

Sharon raised her eyebrows as she related this part of the story, and then said, "But people act funny when they're mad. They stop thinking altogether. I used to do crazy things when I was fifteen."

"Like what?" asked Kelsey.

"Oh, like the time I ran away and rode the T for twelve hours."

"The 'T'?" I asked.

"That's the subway in Boston," Kelsey told me. "Twelve hours on the T? Didn't you get hungry?"

"Oh, I got off now and then to eat and pee. But then I'd get back on, find a window seat and sit there, staring out the window, imagining how worried my parents must have been. It turned out that they didn't start worrying until I'd been gone about nine hours, when I didn't show up for dinner. So I had wasted all those negative thoughts." Sharon always had to put that New Age spin on things.

"Did you get grounded?"

"You know, I don't remember. What I remember most is the look on my mother's face when I got back to the house at midnight. She was scared. Scared and angry. That's a potent combination in a mother. I wouldn't know it myself until Paul was born. Then I understood. Whenever he got hurt as a little kid, and now, whenever he's later than he says he's going to be, I see my mother's face as I walked in the door that night. And I tell her I'm sorry I did that, just in case she's listening."

It was weird to imagine Sharon as a fifteen-year-old, and it was weirder to think that I would be her age someday, looking back and not quite remembering this time of my life. I looked at Kelsey, the sun shining on her blonde hair, the glitter on her shoulders sparkling, the ocean sparkling out beyond us, and wondered if we really would stay friends past this vacation.

"Come on, let's go see some sights." Sharon pushed herself up out of her cross-legged position and walked toward the playground to round up the kids.

* * *

We did some fun stuff to keep the kids from getting bored, and had these little philosophical conversations in between. First we took the shuttle out to the lighthouse. The tour guide said the families that had lived there would have gotten their supplies at the beginning of the winter and then not seen anyone for months.

I tried to picture my family as lighthouse keepers. No one to play with but my brother and sister. No TV of course. No jobs for my parents to get stressed out about. No traffic to get caught in. I figured my parents probably wouldn't have ended up divorced if they'd lived in a lighthouse in the 1800s. But I wasn't sure it would have been worth it.

After that Sharon took us to one of her favorite beaches in Vineyard Haven. The little kids collected shells, starfish, and sand dollars while Sharon told me and Kelsey more about her funny teen years, how she'd come up to the Cape with her parents and stay in Farnsworth House, which was full of college guys working for the summer.

"Each year I'd have a new crush. They were so nice to me when I was little. They'd play hide-and-seek and put on puppet shows for me. But then, there was a time, starting when I was about twelve, when suddenly I couldn't talk to them anymore. I was stunned into silence by how beautiful they were. Overwhelmed by their . . . their *male*ness. So I would sit, all day, and watch them. I used to love to stare at their shoulders from behind. And I would listen when they talked about sports or their jobs, but especially when they talked about girls. I was so quiet, they would forget I was there."

"Research, huh?" asked Kelsey.

"Exactly," nodded Sharon.

"Weren't you lonely?" I asked, imagining this silent girl hiding in the corners of the huge Farnsworth House parlor.

"Well, I guess I was. A little. But I didn't really think of myself as lonely. The guys were fascinating. And I think it did me some good, you know? By the time I was in high school, I was something of an expert in teenage male behavior. I was an only child, but it was as if I had grown up in a house full of brothers. I got over my shyness by the time I was fifteen, and I could talk to them again. My first sexual experience took place during one of those Farnsworth House summers."

Way too much information.

Did I want to know about Sharon's sexual awakening—as my English teacher referred to such things—in Farnsworth House? I thought of the attic room where we slept now, where I'd seen Beka and Paul a few nights ago, and wondered if Sharon had lost her virginity under the attic roof. Was it with one of the guys who'd carved his initials into the wood? Had the bedsprings squeaked? The hardest thing was imagining Sharon, with all her long, gray hair, as a teenage girl.

California Kelsey loved this kind of talk.

"Really? Who was he? Was it wonderful?" And then, in a teasing, parental tone, "I hope you used protection."

"Oh, those boys all had condoms. Carried them around just in case, you know? Of course most of those condoms probably disintegrated in those wallets." She got quiet for a minute and looked out at the water. "I had a friend who got pregnant back then, though. Her parents sent her off to an old aunt's up in Maine and made her give up the baby for adoption. So some of us were unlucky. But yes, my dear, I 'used protection.' I take it your mothers have gone over all that with you?"

"Oh yeah," said Kelsey. "Well, my grandmother. She made it part of our 'Welcome to Womanhood' celebration."

"Good for her!" said Sharon. "You know, some people think if you tell teenagers about safe sex, it's going to make them go out and have sex, right then and there."

"Oh yeah, as if," said Kelsey. "I mean, I'm sitting in a restaurant with my grandmother talking about condoms. Like that's going to make me hot or something."

I did not want to hear this.

In my house, sex education consisted of my mother's handing me a pamphlet about periods on my twelfth birthday. The next morning at breakfast, she asked—in a whisper that got Chris's and Emmy's attention—whether I'd gotten a chance to read it, and whether I had any questions.

"About what?" asked Emmy.

"Girl stuff," said Chris.

"I'm a girl. Tell me!"

"Everybody, eat your breakfast," ordered Mom in what Dad used to call her "take-no-prisoners" tone. Chris went back to reading the comics page and Emmy babbled on about how she was a girl and Mommy was a girl and Tracy was a girl until the question of what Mom and I had been talking about just evaporated. And that was that.

When my period did finally come, it was right during the time she and Dad were trying to work out the divorce settlement. She bought me my supplies, gave me a big hug, and cried. Then kept crying on and off for the next couple of days.

Just a few weeks before this vacation she and I were in the car together when a condom ad came on the radio. "Hmm. Condoms," she said, looking at me. "Honey—"

"Got it Mom. Health class."

"Oh. Okay. Did you have any—"

"Nope. No questions, thanks."

And that was that.

Chapter 16

On the drive home I made a mental list of things to ask Kevin when I saw him again. "Ask them about themselves," the advice columns said, "and they'll talk all night long."

"When did you first start acting?" "What's your favorite subject?" "Do you like going to the beach?" I didn't know how this was going to further our relationship. But I figured if we could just get started again, we'd pick up where we left off at the playground the night before.

"Oh look, someone's at the piano," said Sharon as we pulled into the driveway. "That's just how I want Farnsworth House summers to be. Full of music and laughter."

When I looked at the window all I could see was the reflection of the sunset. Blue sky striped with orange, yellow, and pink. But then just behind that, I could see a silhouette moving back and forth at the piano bench. I wondered if Larry had gotten out the old Beatles' songbook again.

As I closed the car door, I heard music blaring and boisterous male laughter. Halfway to the front steps, I recognized Brett's voice singing "Nighttalk," her first single, the one that had made her so famous:

Who is it
you see when
you say, "no, no, no, no,
don't go, go, go, go"?
Not me. I'm right here.
And I'm not goin'
Nowhere.

"That's perfect! You nailed it!" I heard Kevin's unmistakable voice say.

I hurried up the steps and opened the screen door, excited to hear one of my favorite songs over the Farnsworth House airwaves, and eager to see Kevin again.

I froze. There, in front of the piano, sat Beka, her arms hovering over the keyboard, bent slightly at the elbow. She'd wet her hair, tied it up, and changed into her sleeveless black leotard. She looked so elegant, sitting there with her back straight and her usually slumpy shoulders held out. It was eerie, how much

Beka resembled Brett in the "Nighttalk" video.

Until she moved, that is. In the video, Brett sits at the piano with her eyes closed, and takes these long, deep breaths through her nose. Like in yoga or meditation. But it isn't dopey or anything. All you have to do is watch Brett's face and you can see she's for real. And then, with every keystroke, every nod and tilt of her head, you can see how the music she plays comes out of her, out of who she is.

Beka took all of Brett's signature moves—the breathing, that shoulder shimmy thing she does as she moves into the "Nighttalk" chorus, the way she closes her eyes and raises her chin as she reaches for a note— and made it all look stupid. Like a *Saturday Night Live* sketch. She breathed so heavily through her nose that she snorted, and raised her chin so high she practically did a back bend.

Every move Brett makes at the piano is about the music and the stories her lyrics tell. Every move Beka made was about Beka. Look at me, look at me, look at me.

And they were. Dave and Paul and Chris and especially Kevin were all looking at Beka. They were sitting on the steps next to the piano, staring out through the bars under the banister.

Kevin's eyes were all lit up, and he kept joining in for the little parts in parentheses, punctuating Beka's flat vocals with some pretty cool harmonies, and offering "yeahs" here and "uh-huhs" there.

I let the screen door slam behind me.

Chris, Paul, Dave, and Kevin all turned my way. Beka sat perfectly still. She pulled her hands into her lap and stayed facing the piano. I could only see her from the side, but I was pretty sure the beginnings of a smirk were forming at the edges of her mouth.

Kevin took a deep breath and said, "Hey, you're back," in an oh-so-innocent like he didn't know I loved Brett Smith kind of way. Like he hadn't told me just the night before that he thought she was "one of the most talented singer-songwriters around today." Like he hadn't been talking about how scary Beka was on the ride out this morning.

All I could say was, "Yeah, we're back." I felt my face turn even redder than it already was. I was so shocked, I couldn't think. But I knew one thing: I wasn't going to let anyone—especially Beka—see me cry.

So before any liquid could make its way out of my tear ducts, my feet were moving. I bolted through the parlor, the dining room, the kitchen, and wound up in the pantry, where I helped myself to a big, unopened bag of potato chips. I didn't care who saw me. They could all know it was me siphoning off the M&M's. What difference could it possibly make? And then I ran up the creaky narrow stupid secret stairs to the smelly girls' dorm and plopped myself down on my musty old bed.

By the time the first tear made its way down my cheek and into my mouth, I had ripped the bag open.

At first I took one at a time, letting the salt and grease of the chips wipe out the salt of the tears. Then it was two, three, four in one bite.

I'm not sure which was worse: watching Beka totally trash Brett or watching Kevin aiding and abetting like that.

I lay there, stuffing a new handful of chips in my mouth just as soon as I swallowed the one before. I was in something of a salt-and-grease coma when Kelsey joined me on the squishy mattress. At first she didn't say anything. She just rubbed my back for a while and stroked the back of my head.

Finally, she said, "Come on, Tracy, it's just Beka."

But it wasn't just Beka. I was used to Beka's snotty attitude, and I knew she'd never like me. I tried to explain to Kelsey that it was the way Kevin and Dave and Paul and even Chris were all laughing with Beka that upset me so much. It was like the whole male species was laughing at me.

"Oh come on, they were just fooling around," said Kelsey. "They weren't laughing at you, Tracy. Don't take it so personally."

"How am I supposed to take it?"

"With a sense of humor maybe?"

"Right. Kevin knows how much I like Brett. We talked about it last night. Look." I unbuttoned the top of my overalls to show her the T-shirt.

"Okay, so that doesn't mean—"

"And don't try to tell me that Beka didn't plan the

whole thing, that she wasn't just waiting to show me how easy it was for her to get Kevin's attention."

"But Tracy, you weren't even here. It's not like he was ignoring you. He was just hanging out. They were all just hanging out. Do you know why?"

"Why?"

"They were waiting for us to get back. They're all downstairs now waiting for you and me to come down so we can all go to the playground."

"They're not waiting for me, Kelsey, they're waiting for you."

"They're waiting for *us*," she said.

"Well I'm not going."

"Oh come on, don't be like that. If you don't come, Beka wins."

"Beka already won, Kelsey."

"I really don't think Kevin's interested in Beka."

"Well, maybe you can get him then."

"What? What are you talking about?"

I wasn't sure. All I knew was that I was done watching all the guys drool over Kelsey, the California dream girl. And I wasn't even going to try to compete with Beka, the professional drama queen.

"I'm talking about how you and Beka are like peas in a pod." Getting Kelsey to leave me alone was going to take some drastic action.

"What?"

"You're not happy unless all the male attention is focused on you."

"That is not true, Tracy."

"Yes it is. You're just like Beka. That's why you think what she did is no big deal."

Kelsey stood there for a second, looking bewildered. Then she opened her mouth to say something, but I stopped her. I stopped her by saying what was maybe the meanest thing I've ever said.

"Get out of here, you stupid girl. You are a stupid, stupid girl, Kelsey Wilcox. A dumb, stupid blonde! Get out of here."

That did it. The slightest, softest whimper escaped from the back of her throat and then she closed her mouth. Water welled up in one corner of one eye. But she turned and walked out the door before it went anywhere.

And so there I was, *Alone in the Attic* while *Together Time* continued below.

Someone had turned the music off, but the guys were still booming away. A girl's voice—probably Kelsey's, which was higher than Beka's—said something, and everyone got quiet for a minute. Then I heard the basement door open. Loud, heavy steps down and back up. I could just see Paul with his skateboard under his arm, taking the steps two or three at a time. More voices. The slamming of the screen door. Footsteps down the wooden steps and across the gravel driveway.

I got off my bed and moved to the window, being sure to stay out of sight.

I heard Kelsey say to Beka, "Are you feeling better?"

And Beka said, "Yeah, I guess. Sorry for ruining your day."

Yeah, right.

"Don't worry," said Kelsey, speaking a little bit louder, so that someone listening out the upstairs window might hear. "*You* didn't ruin my day. My day was just fine, up till a minute ago." I didn't hear what Beka said in response, just more footsteps walking across the pebbled driveway followed by more male laughter. I heard Kevin ask something and I thought I heard my name, but by then they were too far away for me to be sure.

Chapter 17 *

Sharon had promised the little kids make-your-own-sundaes after dinner. I heard the freezer door swish open and the thuds of three huge tubs of ice cream being placed on the counter, followed by the thwacks of industrial-sized containers of toppings, sprinkles, whipped cream, and nuts. I distracted myself from my misery by imagining the huge sundae I would make for myself given the chance: one scoop of vanilla with chocolate syrup, one scoop of chocolate with caramel sauce, and a scoop of strawberry with those syrupy strawberries on top.

But the fantasy didn't last. Instead of making my dream dessert I lay there, unable to stop crying and not knowing exactly what I was crying about. There was so much to choose from: I had basically blown my friendship with Kelsey and any chance I might have had with Kevin all in the space of a day, and most of it in only five minutes. And then there was missing my mom and wishing my dad and I could have our Saturday mornings at the deli.

Eventually, I wore myself out and dozed off, only to wake a little later, drenched in sweat and confused. It was dark, and at first I thought it was the middle of the night. But the clock said 8:45, and then it all came flooding back.

The house was quiet. I changed into my army pants and "Power Girl" Brett T-shirt and headed down the pantry stairs, hoping to grab some leftover pizza and maybe even make that sundae I'd been dreaming about. Halfway down, I heard voices, and stopped. Then, avoiding the creaks, I crept step by step until, by craning my neck, I could see Larry and Loraine at the kitchen table, laughing. I hadn't seen any of the parents since we left them back at the carousel earlier in the day, and I wondered where my dad was.

Loraine certainly looked a lot happier than last time I saw her, on the bench in the arcade. Now she was sitting across from Larry, listening as he told the story of how he came to be a real estate magnate. I sat down, back to the wall, making sure I was out of their line of sight, and listened.

"I was in business school. Nan was working as a secretary in a real estate office. Then the owner of our apartment building was going to sell, and the guy Nan worked for said we should buy it. 'Good investment.'

It was cheap. And since it was near the university it would always rent. Her parents loaned us the down payment and the rents covered our mortgage. We had a couple of scary months when an apartment or two stood empty and we'd eat rice and beans. But we always made it. I went to work for a property management firm after I got out of B-school. Learned the ins and outs."

"And one thing led to another and now you're a mogul," offered Loraine. Her tone had definitely changed. Now she was all smiles and admiration. "It's a regular rags-to-riches tale. That's very American, you know. The self-made man thing."

"Well, we're talking fifteen years here. And, you know it wasn't all good. Kelsey was born just as I was going out on my own. We had more lean times, and I had to be away from the house for long days and some nights. Of course, you don't realize it at the time, you're just thinking, 'I've got a family now and I've got to provide for them as best I can,' and then while you're out there trying to earn money so that your family can have a nice life, your family starts falling apart."

"But Josh . . ."

"Oh, yeah, we stuck it out for a while, thinking that things would get better once the business really took off. We went ahead and had Josh, thinking we'd be okay once I didn't have to spend so much time away from the house, and once we had a little money for Nan to get some help with the house and the kids, you know, and once we got the bigger house in the better neighborhood, blah, blah, blah. But things never got okay again, and by the time Kelsey was eleven, the big D had come to call. We were rich, but we weren't us anymore, you know?"

"Yeah, I think I do. My first one was like that. Only without the money."

First one? Loraine was divorced twice?

"It was our careers. Both of our careers. Well, it was his career versus my career, actually. We met in grad school. . . ."

Loraine's story was different from the one I'd imagined for her, Beka, Sammi, and Sean ever since hearing that they lived in Manhattan and that Beka went to the Bellwin School and studied ballet. I figured she was rich and spoiled and that's why she was so mean.

Loraine had wanted to be a writer. When she met Beka's dad, she was working on a novel. She'd won some big grant right out of college, and everyone expected great things from her. Beka's father was studying archaeology. "We had the perfect plan. I would write while he taught his classes. We'd live happily in some quiet college town and spend our summers on digs in exotic places."

But Beka came along before the novel was done. "I had visions of tapping away at the computer with a baby at my breast. Boy was I naïve. I could barely read a newspaper after that. I was supposed to be this big star writer, but I was just a professor's wife. It was all I could do to keep from strangling Beka and swallowing arsenic myself."

Now this was much more information than I bargained for when I sat down to eavesdrop. Hearing it almost made me want to turn around and head back upstairs. But the sneaky snoopy part of me won out, and I sat there on the steps listening while Loraine explained how she got the therapy she needed to get out of her depression, but how it was too late for her marriage, and how she married Sammi and Sean's dad, "Nick-the-artist," too soon after her divorce from Frank, thinking Nick-the-artist's passion for his work would help her rediscover her passion for writing.

They lived in a loft in Brooklyn and she took the job at Beka's school, planning to use the summers to get back to her novel, but of course, that never happened because the twins came along and Nick-the-artist was too busy welding huge sculptures out of discarded household appliances to help her, and there she was again, but this time with three kids and no husband, and a job she liked but which wore her out.

"Do you have any idea what it's like to spend six hours a day, five days a week in rooms full of teenage girls?"

"You should get a medal," offered Larry. So the guy could come up with the right line now and then.

With her salary, child support, and the help of her

parents, Loraine had managed to buy a little two-bedroom apartment on the Upper West Side which was of course way too small now that Beka was fifteen. "I share a room with the twins, so she can have her own space. And still, she hates me." She started to cry again.

The combination of my own troubles and hearing about theirs was almost enough to set me off, too. Not only did I feel bad for Loraine, hearing this story actually made me feel sorry for Beka. Her parents divorced before she turned ten. Then her mom married someone else, had two more kids, and divorced again.

I heard a chair scrape and things got quiet. When Loraine started talking again, it was like her volume had been turned down a couple notches, and I could only hear individual words and phrases in between her mumbling and sniffling.

"Thanks. *Mumble sniffle.* You and Hank *mumble mumble sniffle* great. *Sniffle mumble* Sharon told me sniffle single fathers. Mumble mumble good to see sniffle dads mumble mumble . . ." She blew her nose and continued, "Hank's *mumble mumble* Chris, and worried about Tracy."

Hearing my own name, I had to get closer. I lifted myself from the step I was sitting on, using the walls for support. I felt with my foot for the step below and shifted my weight. But as I eased myself down I slipped and twisted and landed with a thunk. My already scraped knee came down on a nail head that was sticking out from one of the steps.

As if it hadn't done enough damage for one day, my rebellious mouth let out a pretty loud "ouch," and before I knew it, Larry and Loraine were by my side in the darkened stairwell.

"You okay?" asked Loraine as she pulled down the string to light the single bulb at the bottom of the steps. "Oh. That looks bad. Let me clean it up."

She walked across the room to the big first-aid kit that Sharon kept near the stove, and Larry said, "Hey, we thought you guys were all out at the school yard."

So he hadn't heard anything about what had happened.

"Oh, I was so tired," I said, which was true. "I took a little nap." I guess you could call it that. "We did a lot of walking today." Totally true.

Loraine walked back with a brown plastic bottle in one hand and a wad of cotton in the other. "Thanks for helping to take care of the twins. It sounds like they had a great time, despite their sister's antics. Here, come on into the kitchen. Larry, help her get up."

It wasn't until I tried to walk that I realized how much it hurt. Larry lifted me up by the elbow and helped me navigate the three bottom steps, then he led me through the pantry and on to a kitchen chair.

Loraine stood over me. "Gonna have to take those pants off for me to clean you up. Larry, go get me that little blanket Sharon keeps on the parlor couch.

"Yes doc, right away. Wow, I feel like I'm on *ER*." And he started whooping out the *ER* theme music, which made Loraine smile and almost got me to laugh.

Larry was still whooping when he came back in with the blanket. "Here you go doctor. Anything else?"

"Yeah. Turn around and give this patient some privacy."

He did as he was told while Loraine helped me pull my pants over my hips. Some of the fabric was sticking to the blood on my knee, and she lifted it carefully. "Oh. That is a serious cut, young lady. Larry, go look at that nail. I think we might need a tetanus shot here." She threw the blanket across my lap and tucked it up behind me.

"Okay. I think this is the one," he said from the stairwell. "There's definitely some rust here. They're all rusty. We'd better take her in, just to be sure." He walked back into the kitchen, and started scanning Sharon's big bulletin board. "I know I saw the hospital number here somewhere."

"Now this is going to sting, honey, but we have to do it." Loraine looked up at me while she filled the cotton with peroxide.

She was not kidding. That stuff burned.

"Do you know where my dad is?"

"He and Sharon took the little kids to the movies." Loraine went through about five wads of cotton before she got my cut reasonably clean. She looked at my

T-shirt and smiled. "Brett Smith, hey Beka loves her. Or she did. She's into the punk stuff now." She snipped a big square of gauze in half with the little first-aid kit scissors that reminded me of the ones they used to give us in kindergarten. She folded it in half, and then in half again and placed it firmly against my bloody knee. "Hold that. Press it down. That's right." Then she rolled out about a foot of that sticky white tape and cut it into four pieces, which she crisscrossed against my knee. It was the most motherly thing I'd seen Loraine do since I'd met her.

She talked about Beka the whole time she was working. I couldn't tell if she was talking to me, or to Larry, or to herself. I kind of got the feeling that she was talking to Beka, who was probably puffing away at a cigarette by now, doing some wild New York skating moves on Kevin's skateboard.

"Brett Smith was all she listened to. We went to a concert together just last year, in that faraway time when she still let her mother take her places. Ah. Those were the days."

She pressed the last bit of tape in place and said, "Okay, kiddo, we've got to go to the emergency room."

That got Larry going with the *ER* theme again.

"Really, I mean, it's just a cut. I'll be okay."

"Yeah, but those rusty nail cuts can be dangerous." Then, suddenly turning to Larry, she said, "Would you please, please, *please* stop that!?"

He did stop, immediately. "I was just trying to lighten the moment. You don't have to be so mean about it, lady."

"Well, you sound like a sick duck." As she said that, Loraine looked right at me and then we both looked over at Larry, who had turned his lips downward like a pouting baby. We looked back at each other and cracked up.

Chapter 18*

"Pretty professional job there," said the nurse assigned to my knee.

"Thanks," said Loraine. "With three kids, you get the scraped knee thing down."

"Three, huh? That's a lot these days. You're a brave woman."

Loraine smiled at the nurse and then turned to me with a what-does-she-know? look. She and I had been sitting in the waiting room for two hours. Larry had gone back to Farnsworth House, so that someone would be there when the others came home. We made our way through the skimpy collection of well-worn magazines while the doctors and nurses took care of the real emergencies. There was a little kid, maybe three or four, whose hand had been smashed in a car door, and an old man whose neighbor had found him sprawled out on his kitchen floor with a big bloody gash in his head.

"And you did a nice job banging yourself up," the nurse said to me after she'd loosened Loraine's gauze and tape. "How'd you manage that?"

I didn't want to linger on this topic. I was pretty sure that Larry and Loraine had no idea how long I'd been listening to their conversation, but I felt kind of sleazy about it anyway. So I told her what I thought was the same story I'd told them.

"I slept through dinner and woke up hungry, so I was on my way down to the kitchen for a snack. Then I decided I felt cold, so I turned around to run up and get my sweater. Somehow, I missed a step. . . ."

As I said this, I watched Loraine's face for signs of suspicion. I guess it sounded believable. It *was* a little breezy. Loraine had a sweatshirt on. She just nodded at me and looked at the nurse, who continued the nursy small talk.

"So how old are your other two?"

She assumed, as of course anyone would have, that the teenaged girl and the mom-aged woman were mother and daughter.

"What? Oh, Tracy's not mine. I've got one her age though, and six-year-old twins."

"Wow. A teenager and twins. Sounds challenging."

"Yup. It is. It sure is."

*   *   *

We had to call my mom from the hospital to find out about my tetanus shot status. She freaked a little when I first told her where I was, but I talked her down quickly. The nurse got on the phone to discuss the business of the shot, and they decided I should have one just to be safe. Then Loraine asked if she could speak with my mom.

That was weird. I mean, I was pretty sure by then that there was nothing going on between my dad and Loraine anymore—if there even had been anything to begin with—the stuff I'd heard Loraine tell Larry was making me rethink. Still, it seemed weird. But then as soon as they were talking, it was like they were old friends, like Loraine was the mother of one of my old friends or something. "Oh she's fine, Barbara. . . . Yup. . . . Yup. Tracy's a great kid, we've really enjoyed getting to know her, my daughter and I."

Although I had definitely been warming up to Loraine over the day, I thought this was pushing it a little on her part. I mean, as if Beka and I would *ever* be friends. And really, until today, I didn't think Loraine paid much attention to me at all, except maybe as someone who was getting in the way of her interest in my dad.

"Okay. Okay. We will. Oh, it was nothing. I'm sure you'd do the same. Bye, now." She clicked the off button and put the portable phone down next to me. "Your mom sounds nice. I can tell she misses you guys."

The nurse walked back into the room with the shot stuff. Loraine and I watched as she filled the syringe from the little glass vial and turned toward me. "You right handed?"

I nodded.

"Then let's use your left. You might feel a bit bruised tomorrow."

Loraine put her arm around me and said, "You can squeeze my hand if you want."

I was about to say no thanks, that's okay, but then I found myself slipping my hand in hers and squeezing it as hard as I used to squeeze my mom's when I was little. Her skin felt soft, and her fingers were slender like my mother's, and I kind of wished we could stay like that a little longer. Now that my "emergency" was over, we'd be heading back to Farnsworth House where I'd have to face Kelsey—and Beka and Kevin—sooner or later. And as nice as it was to see this other, protective side of Loraine, I didn't think she'd be able to keep it up once we were back there and she had her surly daughter and her psycho son to manage.

* * *

We were just walking out of the examination room when my dad ran up. "There you are. You okay? What happened?"

I filled him in, remembering to tell the story about waking up hungry and deciding to get a sweater exactly the same way I'd said it to the nurse and to Loraine and Larry, but changing a few of the words so that they wouldn't think it was a lie that I was just repeating exactly the same way to throw them off. I had read that that was one way detectives could spot a fake alibi. If the suspect just told the exact story, exactly the same way each time she was asked, like she had rehearsed it or something, then you had to suspect she was lying and you had to put her at the top of your list of possible culprits.

Loraine told Dad about our call to Mom, which he seemed totally cool with, and then he asked if we were hungry.

We found an all-night diner out on the main road. I had scrambled eggs and home fries and would have gone for a chocolate sundae, but those guys didn't want any dessert, so I passed and steeled myself for the return to the scene of my crime.

By the time I dragged myself up the stairs to the attic it was after midnight. I heard voices coming from the girls' dorm. For a second I thought Emmy must be talking in her sleep again. As I got closer, I recognized Kelsey's voice.

"Yeah, and then someone set these fires. . . ."

"At your *school*?"

Every time I'd heard Beka talk so far this summer it had been to say something snotty to me or to fight with her mother or to flirt with Paul. Now she sounded like a normal teenager involved in a normal conversation.

"Your school makes mine sound so boring and tame. One thing happened last year though. These girls got busted for setting up a sex site on the Internet."

"That's creepy," said Kelsey.

"Yeah. They filmed themselves with their boyfriends and then used some of the school equipment to edit it or something, which is how they got caught. One girl's parents sent her off to a convent in Switzerland."

They stopped talking the minute I walked in the room. Kelsey looked at me for a second and turned away.

Compared with that chilly greeting, Beka's seemed positively warm. "Hey. How's your knee?"

"Okay. Your mom pretty much took care of it. But they thought I should get a tetanus shot because of the rust and all."

"They give you any fun drugs?"

"Nah. They told me to take ibuprofen if it hurts."

"That's too bad. When I got my stitches in my arm they gave me Tylenol with codeine. That's fun. You can get buzzed on doctor's orders."

"Yeah? Maybe I should have said it hurt a lot more." I didn't know what I was saying. I'd had some of that codeine stuff a couple of years before when I'd had my tonsils out, and it made me nauseous.

Clearly, the two of them had been getting to know each other a little better while I was stuffing my face and spying on their parents. At first I thought that

Kelsey must be putting on an act, pretending to be Beka's friend just to get back at me. But that was the thing about Kelsey. She really wasn't like that.

Now that I knew more of Beka's story, I found it hard to be so mad at her. And while I wasn't exactly ready to be friends—not that she wanted to be friends with me or anything—I was at least ready to stop hating her. A little.

But Kelsey was not, apparently, ready to stop hating me just yet. "Excuse me," she said coldly, sounding a lot like the old Beka as she walked toward the bathroom with her toothbrush in one hand and her bright plastic banana cosmetic bag in the other. I was sitting on the edge of my bed, and my legs were kind of sticking out. She could have gotten around them without making a big deal of it. But I pulled them up on the bed, and got an even colder, "Thank you."

I wriggled into my sleeping bag and took everything but my Brett T-shirt off and dumped it all on the floor next to me. Then I rolled over, put my hand over my throbbing knee, and tried to sleep.

I heard the rattle of Beka's pill bottle and the rustling of Kelsey's hairbrush before the two of them exchanged friendly good nights and turned out the lights.

Then, for what seemed like hours, my mind proceeded to show an endless replay of the day's events: a close-up of the smile on Kevin's face when we first met that morning, then another of his expression after

I said I didn't want to go feed the gulls, then a super slo-mo version of Beka's flying leap, followed by a quick cut to her smirking at the piano, with Kevin singing "uh-huh, uh-huh," and laughing. Then I'd hear my own voice saying, "stupid, stupid girl" and see Kelsey's mouth open to let that little sound out of the back of her throat.

Eventually, I fell into a half sleep, where I saw it all again.

Chapter 19

I guess I moved around a lot in my sleep, because by morning the scab had broken and bled and then scabbed up again, leaving a gross mess under the gauze. Plus my arm felt like I'd been punched—hard— a few times.

But the knee and arm were nothing compared with what I was feeling in my stomach when I heard Kelsey laughing down in the kitchen.

I smelled coffee and bacon coming up the secret stairs, and heard Paul's and Sharon's voices as well. I didn't know if anyone was in the room with me, and I didn't dare look. I pulled the sleeping bag over my head.

I wanted to go home. I wanted to be in my own bed and have no one to answer to but myself for the day. If I had been home, I would have gone down to the library, gotten a few books, and then walked to the little convenience store next to the park where I'd buy three six-packs of mini powdered doughnuts and a pint of chocolate milk. After a lot of experimentation, I'd concluded that a pint of chocolate milk could last you all the way through eighteen mini doughnuts, as long as you didn't take more than two mouthfuls of milk per doughnut, one to help get you chewing, just after you popped it in your mouth—whole—and one to wash it all down. Then I would sit myself down on my favorite bench—the one that faced a dog run area, one where I could be sure to be safe from anyone my own age—to read and gulp and chew until it was time to baby-sit at the Bernsteins'.

Their three-year-old girl was so cool. And I don't mean in the high school sense of the word. She just kind of loved being herself and being with you even if you were not anyone anyone would remotely have labeled cool at school. We used to spend whole afternoons walking around their back yard, finding sticks and leaves and acting out little scenarios with her dolls.

I was hunkered down in my sleeping bag, so deep into my fantasy day that I could feel the powdered sugar on my lips, when Emmy burst in. "Tracy, Tracy." She started, as usual, by tugging on my toes.

When I didn't respond, she went from tugging my toes to shaking my shoulders and yelling, "Tray-cee. Tray-cee. Wake up." And then she started to sing, "Wake up, wake up, wake up, wake up," another of Mom's good-mood songs.

"Leave me alone!"

Emmy didn't budge. She was used to my morning grumpiness.

"Come on, we're going to the potato chip factory."

I was about to tell Emmy I had a stomach ache, which was kind of true if you counted the churning I felt whenever I thought about all the relationships I'd messed up the day before. Then I remembered that I had a legitimate medical excuse to get out of this excursion.

"Tell Dad my knee still hurts. I don't think it'll be good for me to walk on it." There was some truth there. The nurse had been very specific and serious when she told me how to wash the wound with peroxide and apply antibiotic ointment to avoid infection.

"You tell him. He's right here."

I peeked out from under my flannel cocoon to see my father smiling next to Emmy. "You think it's that bad?"

"Well, I just don't want to be bending and unbending it all day. You know, that gets it bleeding all over again."

"What will you do here all by yourself?"

"Read." I'd been lugging *A Tale of Two Cities* everywhere I went that summer, but hadn't yet made it past the first few pages. "I've got to get ready for my summer reading test." Faced with a medical and an academic reason, he relented.

I stayed upstairs after Dad and Emmy left the

room, hiding in my sleeping bag until after I'd heard successive bangs of the screen door, the crunch-crunch of feet on the pebbled driveway, and the revving of the car engines. I poked my head out into an empty Farnsworth House. Quiet enough to hear the waves lapping.

I wondered if anyone had ever been this alone in all of Farnsworth House's eighty years. The pictures down in the parlor were always so crowded. Rows and rows of people around the piano. The artists from the time of Sharon's grandparents, the college boys from Sharon's teen years, the families from the last few years' Together Times and the other freaks and geeks who came to Sharon's meditation and yoga things.

I found a bagel and a lump of cream cheese on a plate with a knife and glass of juice next to it on the kitchen table. For a minute, I let myself hope that Kelsey had put it out for me. Then I saw an unsigned note, "Bone Appetite," with a paw print at the bottom. The neat, tiny handwriting looked just like the corny signs Sharon had hanging around the house: "Your mother doesn't work here. Please clean up after yourself" over the sink and "Flush, hold, jiggle for 5 seconds (and don't forget to wash your hands!)" above the handle on the toilet. Well, at least someone didn't hate me.

I ate half the bagel with all the cream cheese on it and opened my book to "It was the best of times, it was the worst of times" for the one hundred and fourteenth time. I so wanted to forget everything that had been happening that I read and read and read until the morning sun made its way across the crumb-covered wooden table and out toward the dining room. I got past the part about Madame Defarge's knitting and through three of Lucie's fainting spells. Lucie, the golden girl all the male characters are in love with, reminded me of Kelsey, only a lot more delicate. That was funny, how the girls in books from back then seemed to faint all the time, for the silliest reasons. Sometimes—like when I walked in to find Beka doing her Brett routine—I *wished* it were so easy just to pass out and disappear for a minute or two. But no. I had to remain conscious through all my humiliations.

My private study hall was interrupted by a singsong voice coming through the screen door. "Hello-o? Hello-o? Is anybody here?" The voice was definitely female, but the banging on the door that accompanied it was so insistent, I got a little nervous. I tiptoed over to the archway that separated the dining room from the living room and peeked around the corner to see a woman who looked like she just stepped off the pages of the J. Crew catalogue. She wore khaki shorts and a bright magenta tank top with a lime green straw bag hanging off her shoulder. A cell phone with a perfectly matched magenta snap-on cover had been clipped to the top of the bag. Her lipstick, also the same color as her shirt, was so shiny it made me wish I had my sunglasses.

"Oh, hi there. Is this the Farnsworth Inn? I didn't see a sign, but I think this is the address." She glanced down at her Palm Pilot. I guess I wasn't doing such a good job of staying out of sight.

"Well, um, it's the Farnsworth *House*. There's an inn down the road. I'm not sure what it's called. Witlaw or Willow or something." I looked over her shoulder to see a bright red convertible parked in the driveway with no one else in it.

"No. No. It's definitely Farnsworth. I'm looking for a Mr. Larry Wilcox. And his two children. I believe they're here for the family function thingy. I'm his fiancée, Carolyn Walsh." And with that, Kelsey's stepmother-to-be opened the screen door and let herself into Farnsworth House, allowing me to see how perfectly she'd finished off the outfit with open-toed leather slip-ons and toenail polish that matched the lipstick and tank top.

I could tell she was trying not to, but as soon as she was standing in the parlor, her nose squinched up and she took two little rabbity sniffs of Farnsworth House air. I knew what she was smelling. When we first got there I smelled it too, that mildewy, old-beach-house smell. But now I was used to it. And I kind of liked it.

"Can you show me to Mr. Wilcox's room?"

Apparently, Carolyn had decided that I was the teenage girl working at the Farnsworth House Inn of her hallucination, saving up for college or something. And from the way she was talking, I don't think she thought I was very good at my job. Like I should have offered to show her "Mr. Wilcox's" room, or park her car, or curtsy or something.

"Um . . . Well, I think you should talk to Sharon. She's the owner. They're out for the afternoon. She and Larry and Kelsey, all of them are off on one of the excursions. I'm just here because I'm supposed to stay off my knee." As I said this, I glanced down at the gauze, which had just a little bit of dried red and yellow ooze showing through, which caused Carolyn's little nose to ick up again.

"Oh, well, I see. I'll just . . ." She stopped and looked around the parlor, and into the kitchen where the other half of my bagel still sat, the plate crusty with dried up cream cheese. She glanced over the photos above the piano without showing the slightest bit of interest, looked at her watch, and asked when "Mr. Wilcox and his family" would be back. The dusty grandfather clock in the corner by the main stairs said twelve.

"They said three or four."

"I see. Well." Taking one last look around, she said, "I think I'll go into town. I saw some cute little shops on my way in. Maybe I'll get some lunch. If Mr. Wilcox, I mean, if *Larry* gets back before I do, please don't mention I was here. It's a surprise."

"Okay," I said, not sure whether I'd be keeping the promise implied. I mean, how could I not tell Kelsey that her dad's girlfriend had shown up all of a sudden unannounced? Kelsey was my friend, right?

So far I'd managed not to think too hard about that question. Looking back at my outburst, I was baffled. I didn't really think Kelsey was stupid. It was just the easy, obvious thing to say to the pretty, blonde—and let's not forget rich—girl who had guys drooling wherever she went. I was a jealous cliché.

An angry girl.

I wandered around the parlor, mulling this over, eventually sitting down at the piano. I started tracing the keys with my index finger. Then I tested a few. It could have used a tuning, but it wasn't totally unplayable. I did some scales. Soon I found myself going through a whole set of Mrs. Finch's warm-up exercises. And then, before I knew it, I was using both hands and the pedals, trying to remember all the verses to "Last Night at the Lake."

But I had to stop after the first verse, because now I could never sing that song or even hear it without thinking of Kevin, and how he sang it so casually that night at the playground.

So I just started messing around, trying to make up my own melody and words. Of course whenever I did that, my songs ended up sounding like rip-offs of Brett Smith songs. Uncle Steve had told me not to worry about it, that that was the best way to learn how to do any kind of art—to imitate the artists you admired.

This one was called "Playground":

You touched me
And you started a fire (I sang it like "fi-ya")
Started the flames.
Now it's roaring, roaring inside me. . . .

Nothing came after that, so I sat there, singing those four lines over and over for a while. I thought about Kevin, how it felt to have his hands on my waist during the skateboard lesson, how he held my hand while we walked across the playground. I closed my eyes and saw him smiling at me that first time Kelsey and I met him and Dave at Plimoth. My eyes got kind of hot, like I was going to cry.

I was starting to wonder how anyone ever finished a song like this, about a real-life experience of love gone bad. How could you be creative and too sad to live at the same time? I kept playing those few lines over and over again, watching the quick-cutting video montage of my "relationship" with Kevin on a continuous loop in my brain. Then a weird thing happened.

I got bored.

So I decided I'd try to make up my own song, one that wasn't so obviously just like "Last Night at the Lake," or so obviously about Kevin, either. That meant putting him out of my head, which wasn't exactly easy, but not impossible. I mean, we'd only had a few little moments. Not a lot of material for a video montage.

I closed my eyes and let myself feel the keys under

my fingers. Sharon's piano was as old as the house, built back when they still used ivory, unlike our piano at home, which had plastic keys. Mrs. Finch had explained the whole story to me, about how for the sake of the elephants in Africa, piano makers had to stop using ivory. I hadn't thought it could be that big a deal, what the keys were made of. But sitting there with my eyes closed, thinking about the elephants and a little bit about Kevin, and a lot about Kelsey, who I missed more than I thought it was possible to miss a friend you'd really just made, the keys did feel different. Smooth and cool and inviting. Maybe it was just because I hadn't been playing for such a long time. In any case, I started to feel a song bubbling up from inside of me.

I could almost see the words as they made their way out of my heart or my stomach or wherever they came from. This was about fire, too, but a whole different kind.

I strike the match
I hear the sizzle,
I feel the heat get hot. . . .
I watch the flames
Dancing their red dance
Against the dark of night.

At first I thought that since they were both about fire, I could make the two fragments into one song.

But then I realized that wouldn't work. "Playground" was about love fire, the fire between two people and this one, which I decided to call "Firedance," was about the burning inside yourself. The energy that helped you write songs or play the piano or whatever it was you did well. They'd be back-to-back tracks on my debut CD, "campfiregirl." A traditional love song followed by a girl-power track.

Now *that* was weird. The way I just suddenly started thinking like my old self again. Like I was that girl who used to sit around writing songs, dreaming of a future life in a downtown loft big enough to hold a grand piano and a recording studio.

I got up to look for paper and pen. I wanted to make sure I got the words down before I forgot. Sharon had a box of scrap paper cut from junk mail and take-out menus. Recycling was a must at Farnsworth House. I grabbed a stack and headed back to the piano. Before I could sit down, though, I heard a car pull into the gravel driveway.

The grandfather clock said one-thirty. Too early for everyone to be back. It had to be Carolyn, done with the cute little shops and checking to see if "Mr. Wilcox" had returned. I knew from past experience that if you didn't get things like songs and poems in your head down on paper right when you thought of them, they'd never come back. And I wasn't going to let someone like J. Crew Carolyn ruin my artistic moment, so I ran out to the kitchen where I was sure no one could see me from the front door and started writing furiously.

I got through all four lines of the playground song and partway through the other one before the knocking at the door ended. When the car door slammed and the engine started, I headed back to the piano to finish.

*   *   *

Two hours later, I felt like a new person. Or rather, like the person I used to be before everything got so hard. It wasn't like I thought that writing a couple of songs was going to make my life all perfect or anything, or get me a record deal for that matter. But still, I felt better. Hopeful and kind of happy.

And strong enough to swallow my pride and try reaching out to Kelsey. I didn't feel quite as awful about myself as I had the night before, lying inside my sleeping bag while she and her new friend Beka drifted off to sleep. I felt guilty still, of course. Because I'd been incredibly mean, as mean as Beka'd been to me. But the hopeful feeling made me think maybe Kelsey would forgive me. So I dialed her cell phone.

"What do you want?" was her first, icy response.

"Um. Well, there's something I thought you'd want to know."

"What?"

"Your stepmother's here."

"My who? What? Carolyn?"

"Yeah. Well, she's not here right now. She went shopping. She was just here a little while ago. She's looking for your dad. She said she was going to surprise him."

"Hah! Check up on him is more like it! She is such a sneak. Does anyone else know?" By now she sounded almost like before, almost like she wasn't mad at me or hurt or anything. Almost like she trusted me.

"No, Kels, I'm the only one here."

"Has Kevin come by?"

"What? No."

"Oh, 'cause he said he was going to come by to talk to you. He called this morning when you were asleep."

I thought of the knocking at the door and the car in the driveway.

"Gee, thanks for telling me." My tone probably wasn't the best for begging forgiveness.

"Uh, I didn't see you. And besides, I was mad at you. In case you don't remember, you were pretty mean yesterday."

"Yeah. I'm really sorry about that, Kelsey. I don't know what got into me."

"You were upset."

"Yeah. I was. Thanks for understanding." I was surprised at how easy it was to make up and was starting to look forward to her coming back.

But then she continued. "You know, Tracy, you're not the only one with issues."

"Huh?"

"I mean, open your eyes. Everyone at Farnsworth House has problems. Some are even bigger than yours."

"You mean Beka."

"Yeah, well, Beka for one. Sharon's right, she *is* a troubled soul. But maybe she has her reasons. She's really not bad once you get past the anger."

I pictured Beka sitting in her leotard at the piano, breathing those big, snorting breaths through her nose. I thought of how she'd always looked away from me rather than acknowledge my presence. But then I remembered everything I heard Loraine tell Larry about what Beka's life had been like.

Still, I wasn't quite ready to forget everything and share Kelsey with her.

"That doesn't excuse her from being civil."

"Yeah, well, what's your excuse?"

*　　*　　*

I hung up the phone with Kelsey's question ringing in my ear.

But then Carolyn banged on the door and started in with her little "Hello-o? Hello-o?" I should have known that the quiet knocker wasn't her.

I let her in, and suggested she wait in the parlor, figuring that's what a woman like her would expect from a servant like me, if I were an actual servant, which she still seemed to think I was. "Why don't you have a seat in the parlor—um—" I almost said, "ma'am," but I just couldn't bring myself.

I gestured to the loveseat under the portrait of Sharon's grandparents. It must have been done by one of the less talented painters of the Farnsworth House salon days. Mr. and Mrs. Farnsworth were sitting in these big, high-backed chairs, with identical ribboned pug dogs in their laps. I guess that was supposed to make them look royal or something. But their eyes were all bugged out, and they looked like hypnotized aliens holding mutant insects.

Carolyn sat there sneezing, looking at her watch, and sighing these big I-don't-have-time-for-this sighs.

Chapter **20**

That night Larry asked Sharon for directions to "the fanciest, most expensive restaurant in town" and by morning Carolyn and the red convertible were gone.

"What was she even doing here?" asked Beka.

"Well, she *said* she had to run some menu ideas by my dad for the wedding. But that was just an excuse to check up on him. I think he may be starting to get cold feet."

"I'd think he'd have frostbite by now," said Beka.

At first it was weird, all three of us sitting around the attic, Beka acting like a normal human being. Who knew she was so funny? Turned out there was a lot I didn't know about her.

Like what it was like to be a relatively poor girl in a rich girls' school.

"Teachers' kids go free," she explained. She told us how she only had one real friend at school, a girl from uptown, Valeria, who was also on scholarship. All the other girls in their class were super rich. Like two or three, and, in one case, four homes rich. Like multiple credit cards with unlimited clothing allowances rich. Like two-month European vacations rich.

Meanwhile, it was all Loraine could do to scrape together enough for Farnsworth House. Beka wasn't even supposed to have come originally. She and Valeria were supposed to go to this dance camp in upstate New York, but Beka's therapist advised Loraine not to let Beka go anywhere on her own.

Her one and only boyfriend—who she'd been with for "a year and seven months and five days"—broke up with her in the spring, and for two weeks she'd refused to leave her room. The pills were antidepressants.

"At least now I can get out of bed in the morning."

Once Beka started telling us about her reasons for being so mean, she stopped actually being so mean. She and Kelsey and I hung out on the beach that afternoon, talking. At first we just talked about our parents, the safe subject. Beka said I should demand that my father make time for my Saturday piano lessons, and that I should try to talk more with my mom.

"Okay," I said. "If you start talking more with yours."

She shrugged.

"She's really worried about you." Suddenly I was the founding member of the Loraine Fan Club.

"Yeah, I know." Beka shrugged again and looked out at the water.

Things were still a little awkward between us until we finally talked about the not-so-safe subject, a.k.a. the Brett Episode, and she admitted that it wasn't just this innocent, spontaneous thing.

"My mom was haranguing me all week about my attitude, pointing to you two as examples of girls who managed to behave 'in spite of life's challenges.'" Beka had Loraine's schoolteacher lecture style down. "Plus, I was totally humiliated when the guys ganged up on me about my Dead Kennedys T-shirt and you two kept exchanging your little looks."

Kelsey and I looked at each other again.

"Don't try to deny it, you know you did."

Now it was our turn to shrug. She was right.

"So I decided to spread the humiliation around a little. I mean, it wasn't like I thought, 'Oh now what would be the best way to hurt someone today?' Well, maybe it was something like that. But see, when I get angry, it kind of takes over."

I knew what she meant.

Beka swore she wasn't interested in Kevin.

"He likes you. It's so obvious."

"Yeah?"

"Yeah. Anyone can see it," Beka said.

"Except you," added Kelsey.

"So why hasn't he tried talking to me?"

"He's scared," said Kelsey.

Now that was ridiculous. "Oh, please."

"Tracy, think about it. You haven't talked to him since you stomped through the living room and refused to come back down. Everybody in the house heard you yell at me. You were scary." Kelsey's version put things in a new light. "Besides," she added. "He did try talking to you. He called you yesterday, and came over here in the afternoon and got ignored."

"But I wasn't ignoring *him*. I was ignoring Carolyn. If I'd known it was Kevin knocking on the door I'd have answered it." Of course, if I'd answered the door, I might not have written my songs. That was a weird thought.

"Face it Tracy, you intimidate him," said Beka.

Now this was too funny.

*   *   *

That night a big thunderstorm kept the guys from their usual after-dinner skating session. Kelsey and Beka and I were shooting pool when they all piled in, dripping with rain and sweat. I thought I was tongue-tied with Kevin before. After hearing everything Beka and Kelsey had to say, I was so nervous I could barely get myself to look at him. When I finally did, he was looking right at me. And he kept looking at me.

"Hey," he said, with a little nod.

"Hey." I thought of my ridiculous list of interview questions and smiled to myself.

I got a big smile back. This communication thing was so weird.

Kelsey opened up the closet with the old board games. After a quick game of Scrabble in which my triple word score for "zither" put me too far ahead for anyone to catch up, we broke out Clue, and Beka had this great idea of inventing all-new suspects and weapons and then redrawing the board to look like Farnsworth House.

Paul ran upstairs for the recycling bin, and we combed through the catalogues and magazines for faces we thought matched our characters. For an hour or so we were like a bunch of preschoolers, totally caught up in our little arts and crafts project.

Chris created "Miss Biddlebottoms, Mayflower descendant with a history of her own," which he illustrated with a middle-aged, diamond-necklace-wearing model from a Tiffany ad.

I cut out a picture of this smiling, floppy-hatted gardener from one of Sharon's seed catalogues and called her "Carey Sunshine, a sixties hippie lost in the twenty-first century."

Kevin grabbed a few markers and scurried off into a corner, where he sat drawing for a few minutes before introducing "Stacy Woods, red-haired singer-songwriter extraordinaire." He had made a simple line drawing of a girl with hair about my length at a piano that looked a lot like Sharon's upright. The girl wore overalls and leather strapped sandals, with painted toenails. Beka and Kelsey looked my way with raised eyebrows, and my heart beat so hard I was sure every-one could hear it.

The new weapons consisted of a skateboard (Dave's idea), a cell phone (Kelsey's), and a frying pan (Paul's). Everyone cracked up when our first murder turned out to be committed by Ms. Sunshine in the pantry with the frying pan.

*   *   *

Kevin and I didn't get the chance for a one-on-one conversation till the next night, when Kelsey and Dave went for a walk on the beach and Chris and Beka were outside smoking and Paul was helping his mom mix up the Farnsworth House granola.

We sat on the loveseat under the Farnsworth founders' portraits.

"So about the other night . . ." Kevin started.

"Yeah?" I took a deep breath.

"Why'd you go so nuts? I mean, it was just Beka being Beka."

Because I thought you thought Beka being Beka was more interesting than Tracy being Tracy. That's just what I thought, not what I said.

What I said was, "I don't know. I hadn't talked

to you since the ferry. It looked like you and Beka were . . ."

"Wait a minute, wait a minute. You blew me off on the ferry."

"What?"

"How soon they forget," he said, looking up at Mr. Farnsworth's portrait. "I asked you to come feed the seagulls and you totally blew me off."

"I did not blow you off."

"No? What do you call it when you ask someone to do something with you and they say 'no'?"

"But I didn't mean . . . I wasn't blowing . . ." So maybe Kelsey and Beka were right. Maybe I had been sending signals I didn't mean. "I'm sorry. I just. I just didn't know how to talk to you. I didn't know what to say and so I said 'no,' but I was hoping you'd kind of stay around, just stand next to me or something until I figured out what to say."

"And how was I supposed to know that, huh? ESP? Ever heard of 'No means no?' You blew me off, Tracy Forrester. And then you ignored me. And then Beka ran away and someone had to find her."

He explained how when they brought Beka back things exploded. She and Loraine got into a "mega-mother-daughter screamfest" and Beka had cried for the whole ferry crossing and then slept all the way through the car ride home.

"We had no idea what to do with an upset Angry Girl. She was practically catatonic when we got back to the house. So when she started that stuff at the piano, we were like, 'hey that's cool.' Believe me, the last thing I was thinking about at that moment was trying to hurt your feelings."

It made sense. Sort of. I still couldn't believe he would think I was blowing him off. Obviously, I was never going to be one of those girls like Kelsey, who could send subliminal double messages like "no's" that really meant "yes," and "go aways" that really meant "stay right here." If I wanted Kevin to understand me, I was going to have to say what I meant.

So I said, "Sorry."

And he said, "Sorry."

And we sat there quietly for a few mintutes, just kind of breathing next to each other while Sharon and Paul banged around in the kitchen. Then Kevin put his hand over mine and, nodding toward the piano, said, "Play something."

And instead of saying no, pretending I didn't want to, like an expert flirt would, to get the guy to beg, I said, "Okay," and walked over to the piano. Kevin slipped onto the bench and sat right next to me. Somehow, in spite of the fact that this really nice, really cute guy was sitting so close I could feel the heat coming off his skin, I played my best.

We made it about halfway through "Last Night at the Lake" before kissing.

Well, it started with nuzzling, which, by the way, is a way more intense phenomenon than its innocent name suggests. Kevin leaned his face into my neck and rested his lips right below my ear. I tried to keep playing, but feeling his breath on my neck like that made it impossible. I just had to turn my face to his. Which led to our lips connecting. Once, twice, lightly—with breaths in between. And then, by the third, our tongues got involved and that hot-and-cold-at-the-same-time feeling came back, along with a new feeling that had a lot in common with what happens in your stomach when you jump off a high dive.

We didn't stop until the screen door slammed. When we untangled ourselves we found Dave and Kelsey holding hands and looking at us.

"Took you long enough," said Dave.

"I was beginning to wonder," added Kelsey.

Chapter 21

Kissing Kevin wasn't the best thing about what turned out to be my not-so-terrible time at the Hippie Hotel. It was just one of the best things.

Another best thing was that he and I started to play music together. The next night, he brought over his acoustic guitar and we worked out a new arrangement for "Last Night at the Lake," using a faster tempo than Brett does on the album. Playing that song together finally ended all the lingering weirdness of the Brett Episode, especially after Beka came down the parlor stairs and started choreographing a dance. For someone who had supposedly outgrown her Brett Smith phase, she looked pretty inspired.

Sharon poked her head in from the kitchen and stood listening and watching for a while, which led to another of the best things: She announced there'd be a talent show the last night—which was just two nights away. She said, "Everyone, and I mean every one of you—kids and grown-ups alike—who wants a seat at our final Farnsworth House family dinner, has to do something."

*　*　*

When Larry heard about the talent show, he asked to be excused on account of his being "totally, utterly talentless. Really, ask my kids." He even said he'd be happy to make a sizable donation to the Farnsworth House scholarship fund "in lieu of participation."

To which Sharon responded, "Everyone on this earth has some unique talent, Larry Wilcox of Wilcox Enterprises. You have forty-eight hours to figure out what yours is, or no supper. Oh, and I'll take that donation. There are a lot of single mothers out there who can't afford to come to Farnsworth House."

*　*　*

For the next forty-eight hours Farnsworth House turned into a big rehearsal studio. People teamed up in obvious and not-so-obvious ways, practicing in secret behind closed doors.

Finally, after a fabulous final dinner of lobster, clams, corn on the cob, and peach cobbler, we gathered in the parlor.

Kelsey and Chris were first. They'd been rehearsing very quietly back in Paul's room, bragging about how they were going to steal the show in spite of the fact that they couldn't sing, act, or play any instruments.

Chris came down the parlor stairs first, wearing jeans and the Navy Deals T-shirt turned inside-out with two big Ms written in glittery nail polish. He had tied a dark blue towel around his neck as a cape. Without cracking a smile, he nodded at the audience and then sat facing us in one of those straight-backed chairs from the Farnsworth portraits.

Then Kelsey clomped down, wearing her bathing suit and some incredibly high-heeled glittery shoes she'd found at the thrift shop in town. She must have used up every last drop of her glitter lotion, because she was positively sparkling. She looked beautiful, which was pretty much how she looked all the time, but she also looked funny, like an exaggerated version of a magician's "lovely assistant."

Kelsey did all the talking.

"Welcome ladies and gentlemen. Tonight you are going to witness the talents of Marvin the Magnificent, a man with a unique talent, an ability no other human being on earth possesses. May I have a volunteer from the audience to assist us in our demonstration?"

"Ooh. Ooh. Pick me. Pick me." All the little kids had their hands up, but it was Sean who was the loudest. I think Kelsey picked him just so he'd shut up.

"Okay. Young man. Now, what am I holding in my hand?"

"M&M's. Yum!" said Sean, reaching for the unopened bag.

"That's right. Hold on a minute there," Kelsey grabbed it back and then she and Sean had a little tug-of-war. All the while she kept her lovely young assistant smile. "Please, young man. Marvin the Magnificent needs your cooperation."

"Let—go—now, Sean," said Loraine as firmly as I'd heard her say anything the whole time we'd been at Farnsworth House, "or you're going upstairs for the rest of the show." Sharon had convinced Loraine to read some of her materials on effective parenting, and she'd been experimenting with this clear rules and real consequences thing. He'd thrown a few tantrums in response, but Loraine had been holding her ground, and he was actually starting to behave.

"Okay," he grumbled. "I was just trying to make the show more fun."

"Yeah, well, you guys will have your turn next."

Kevin and Dave had been working with the little ones on their *Wizard of Oz* production. We were all dreading it, but the guys promised it would be way better than we expected.

"Okay." Kelsey resumed the act. "Now, young man, if I were to open this bag, and place a single M&M on your tongue, would you be able to identify its color without looking?"

"Maybe. I don't know."

"Let's try. Now close your eyes." As Sean stood there squeezing his eyes closed, Kelsey ripped open the bag, pulled one out, and held it up for us to see. Red.

She placed it in Sean's mouth. He pursed his lips, and then moved them back and forth like he was working up a good mouthful of saliva. The room went silent as we sat and waited.

"Okay. Young man," said Kelsey, "what color M&M are you eating?"

"Um. Yellow?"

Kelsey shook her head, still smiling. "What color, audience?"

We all shouted "red," and Sean begged for another chance.

"No, no, thank you very much for your participation. Here's a little token of our appreciation," said Kelsey, pouring a few more M&M's into his hand. For a second Sean looked like he was going to make trouble, but he caught his mother's eye and she gave him this look, and he went back to his seat.

Kelsey made a big show of blindfolding Chris, waving around a tacky, glittery scarf she'd gotten at the thrift store and then rolling it up and wrapping it around his head. Then he successfully identified a yellow, a blue, and a red M&M, taking several sips from a glass of water she held up to his mouth in between to clear his palate.

I still have no idea how he does that.

Originally, Loraine and Larry and my dad were going to do a one-act play adapted from Loraine's novel in progress, but it got too complicated and so they decided to do a game show spoof instead.

Larry played the goofy host perfectly. He'd done his hair in a really weird side part and put a lot of greasy-looking mousse in it, so it was big and stiff. Loraine made fun of herself as a know-it-all contestant who gets really crazy when she can't think of all the original members of the Rolling Stones. My dad pretended to be this little nerdy guy who really does know everything, and who ends up being strangled to death by Loraine's crazed character when he successfully names Mick, Keith, Brian, Bill, and with his final breath, Charlie.

Beka danced while Kevin and I played our up-tempo version of "Last Night at the Lake." As the music came through me and out my fingers, I watched it come out of Beka's feet and arms. When Beka dances, her whole body gets involved. Her neck, her eyes, even her hair dances. All the edginess disappears, too, and it's like there's a light coming off her.

The little kids—including Josh—did their "W.O.O. Revue," a three-minute version of *The Wizard of Oz.* Dave and Kevin narrated so quickly they sounded like auctioneers, while the littles ran around miming the scenes as if they were on fast-forward. Every once in a while someone would shout out part of a key line like "your little dog, too," and "good witch, bad witch?"

and "not in Kansas" and "Pay no attention" etc.

Then Paul and Dave did a cooking demonstration, like they were on the Food Channel. Chris played camera man. Dave worked silently while Paul talked. In French. All they made was a peanut butter and jelly sandwich, but Paul added all these digressions about how peanut butter was made and where strawberries were grown, which, in French, made the procedure sound a lot more serious and complex. He kept shaking his finger into the imaginary camera saying things had to be done "ex-act-e-ment." They wore really tall homemade chef's hats, and neither of them cracked a smile the whole time.

Sharon laughed so hard she cried. And then she took them both in her arms and gave them a big hippie hug.

Kevin and I did a little duet of Brett's "Summergirl" and "Under Your Breath."

Then I debuted "Firedance." I closed my eyes and felt the ivory and invited the feeling—that sense of possibility—that had visited me days before when I sat at the piano all alone. And it came.

I couldn't see anyone's face while I was singing, because the piano is up against the wall and they were all behind me. But when I was done, everybody clapped for what seemed like a long, long time.

Sharon said I had "a true talent" that was my "responsibility to nurture and develop."

To which Loraine added, "Absolutely."

"You'll have to come back for the artist's retreat next year," offered Sharon.

Maybe I would.

Dad came up and hugged me, and said, "First Saturday in September, we're getting you back to Mrs. Finch's, okay?"

"Okay," I said, wondering if he'd follow through.

"Bagels and coffee first."

"Okay . . ."

"This is a promise," he said, taking my hand and squeezing it, and making me look into his eyes. "We'll have a standing date. Just you and your dad."

"Okay. Okay." I squeezed his hand back. Maybe he would.

Kelsey hugged me and said, "Don't forget me when you're famous."

Then Beka hugged me and said she'd like to get together when we're home. Maybe she and Valeria could choreograph something to "Firedance" for their school talent show.

Kevin hugged me and added a little kiss that landed on my neck and made me turn even redder than I already was, listening to all those compliments. He whispered, "Three hours and forty-seven minutes."

Before I could ask him what he was talking about, Sharon made me sing "Firedance" again, this time with everyone standing around behind me so that she could climb up the stairs and take a picture. Kevin slid in next to me at the bench and whispered, "By train. We're only three hours and forty-seven minutes apart."

Only. Nice word.

"Less if we meet in the middle," he added.

Sharon said she was going to put my picture up above the piano, next to the one of the girl from the twenties. The one who went to Broadway.

Everyone said they liked the song. But they're obviously biased.

They're my friends.